I0675073

THE QUEEN'S BEAST

E. MARIE

AUTHOR NOTES

THERE ISN'T MUCH I CAN SAY ABOUT THIS STORY
WITHOUT GIVING AWAY TOO MUCH
INFORMATION - THE ONLY WAY TO UNDERSTAND
IT IS TO READ IT FOR YOURSELF ULTIMATELY. I
ENJOYED WRITING IT, BUT AS WITH ANYTHING IN
MY LIFE I FEEL LIKE I COULD HAVE DONE BETTER.
BECAUSE OF THIS I WOULD LIKE TO THANK K.G.
LONG FOR GIVING ME THE OPPORTUNITY AND
INSPIRATION TO PUT MY WRITING OUT THERE
LIKE THIS. WITHOUT HIM I WOULD HAVE NEVER
BELIEVED IN MYSELF ENOUGH TO DO ANYTHING
LIKE THIS, AND WOULD STILL JUST BE WRITING
FOR FUN IN MY HOUSE LATE AT NIGHT

THERE ARE A FEW MORE PEOPLE I WOULD LIKE TO
THANK AS WELL:

JAMES F.
REX
MICHAEL T.
HONEY

THANK YOU FOR BELIEVING IN ME AND STICKING
WITH ME TIL' THE END.

THIS IS A WORK OF FICTION. NAMES, CHARACTERS,
PLACES, AND INCIDENTS EITHER ARE THE PRODUCT
OF THE AUTHOR'S IMAGINATION OR ARE USED
FICTITIOUSLY. ANY RESEMBLANCE TO ACTUAL
PERSONS, LIVING OR DEAD, EVENTS, OR LOCALES IS
ENTIRELY COINCIDENTAL.

COPYRIGHT © ERIKA M. SPONTARELLI, 2021

ALL RIGHTS RESERVED. NO PART OF THIS BOOK MAY
BE REPRODUCED IN ANY FORM ON BY AN
ELECTRONIC OR MECHANICAL MEANS, INCLUDING
INFORMATION STORAGE AND RETRIEVAL SYSTEMS,
WITHOUT PERMISSION IN WRITING FROM THE
PUBLISHER, EXCEPT BY A REVIEWER WHO MAY
QUOTE BRIEF PASSAGES IN A REVIEW.

FIRST EDITION, SEPTEMBER 2021

PUBLISHED BY COALESCENCE PUBLISHING, LLC
AUTHORS@COALESCENCEPUBLISHING.COM

Chapter One

It was a normal, dark night – dreary some would say as the rain tapped gently against the window. She liked this kind of weather, it was one of the few things she could still appreciate after the accident – this calm during the storm. She could hear it though, a group of angry people marching up to her home atop the hill; the gentle glow reflected off the gate as they made their way to the door, and at the same time the only man she would call her friend – the only one that shared the affliction she'd caused to herself – approached her from across the room. With distant eyes as bored as her own he stood next to her chair – the glow from the fireplace making their shadows dance on the walls and ceiling above as he moved to look out the window – watching those people make their way into the lower portion of the house.

"It appears you've been found out." He said dryly as he quietly peeled the curtain back for a better view. "Shocking." Her friend added with dry sarcasm.

"No one likes an 'I told you so,' Louis." She would say as she pushed herself up from her seat.

"What will you do, Lady Mauvais?" He asked, watching her carefully and arching a brow when she shrugged with a smirk.

"What is there to do? I was caught red handed." She added, buttoning her shirt – male's attire. It was more comfortable than the drab they force women to wear in public.

"Quite literally, Madam." Louis said. His eyes drifted towards the door, the sound of an angry group growing ever closer.

"I can't help the head popped off as I was trying to pull the girl from her grave, nor did I expect the Inspector to show up when he did. That blood soaked through my favorite shirt too, bloody hounds." She said, waving her hand. "Either way, what is there to do? Burn me at the stake?" She laughed and shook her head.

"You're rather calm for a woman about to be taken to trial." He said just as the door began to bow and strain against however many people were charging it on the other side.

"I've done some experimenting, I know there is nothing they can do to hurt me my dear Lou-Lou." She said, tapping his cheek gently. "Or to you, but for all they know you're oblivious in all of this. For all they know you're merely a butler here." She sighed softly. "Just keep an eye on everything while I'm gone. I'll be back." She finished as she turned towards the door.

"Of course Madam." He said, placing a gloved hand over his chest as he bowed his head slightly. "I will be sure the manor is kept to your standards." He added, watching with a dry gaze as she opened the door.

The others gasped, and each took a collective step back as she moved into the hallway. Short black hair against lightly tanned skin, despite her newly garnered reputation she was still beautiful. "Did it ever occur to you fools to knock?" She asked, and was greeted by the head of city enforcement who approached with two of his men, shackles in hand. "That will be unnecessary. I have no intentions of resisting." They all looked shocked. "No point when I was blatantly caught." Her smirk stretched over her lips as she walked past them and down the stairs.

Each one followed, no words were spoken, but she could feel the intensity in the air. Like electricity before a storm. They all wanted her dead, but the sad truth, for them anyway, was that would never happen. Just like with most things these days she blacked out, the boredom must have been too great, because next she knew she was already in a cell. Cold and drab with cobblestone walls, rusted metal bars holding her in. She couldn't help but chuckle to herself at some of the comments Lou-Lou would have made could he see the state of this place. She wondered how long it would take for them to realize that nothing they could do to her would harm her, not even a guillotine could stop her, though it would be annoying to reattach her head for the second time – it's awkward trying to work a surgery like that given one's own head lies on the table. She was shaken from her own thoughts when she heard the heavy metal door open and smash against the wall, the familiar clinking of chains followed by quick hobbled steps.

"Wilhelm, it's been too long." She said before he even stood in front of her cell.

"That's Inspector Goddard to you, murderer." He said with a cold tone, but she could see the fear in his eyes.

"My dear, Wilhelm, it wasn't but two nights ago we were sharing tea in my lounge. Have you so easily dropped me from your heart?" His body was stone, but his eyes trembled like an animal trapped in a cage. "Oh well, it can't be helped I suppose." She would shrug and stand, slowly approaching the cell door. "I am sorry about your friend, but truth be told he should have never tried to play the hero." The fear faded into anger and slowly she placed her hands through the slot and he slapped the shackles to her wrists.

"In the name of our Queen you will face judgment for what you've done." He said through gritted teeth, trying so hard to remain professional in front of his colleagues.
"Afterwards your punishment will be passed down, and for the sake of my dear friend Thomas...I hope it's painfully slow." He added, slowly opening the cell for her to step out.

She had a coy grin as she exited. "I hope so as well." She would steal a glance at him. "What fun is there to be if there isn't even a bit of pain?" She would calmly walk ahead of them, that coy smirk ever etched on her features.

Another carriage ride. The sun was rising over the ocean, time seemed to move much quicker these days. Her assumptions were correct, there was a sea of people waiting in front of the courthouse, likely family and loved ones of those she desecrated over the past three years. So much she'd learned from those participants, so much that was yet to be learned from them. She hoped this would be quick, and she hoped more for their quick defeat on the matter, though she didn't expect to go home without some form of punishment. Likely how this would end is she would end up with an around-the-clock watch, all comings and goings from her manor would be with escort or openly with an armed guard. Annoying, but it couldn't possibly last forever.

"Alright boys, surround her and don't let anyone near her." Wilhelm said with a gruff tone, the other three men in the carriage simply nodded.

"Aw, you do care." She stated with a sickly sweet tone.

"Shut up." He barked, pushing the door open.

The crowd bellowed obscenities towards her, some dared to throw rocks at her feet. She didn't care for these lowly people, none of them held a candle to her family name – well, save perhaps one in attendance. Her eyes locked with the young woman's in the crowd, blond wavy hair cascaded down her shoulders, a black dress and veil, as though she were attending a funeral. She was pale as a ghost, at least what J'ai could make out of her anyway, a stark comparison to the lively smile and bright eyes she normally carried. She stood out remarkably from this crowd of lowlifes, wearing despair rather well. She was ushered into the building, Wilhelm reluctantly grabbing her by the elbow; though it was clear he wanted nothing to do with touching her, it was amusing how quickly some people turned on others. She used to think he was one of the few she could have trusted, luckily she never made any outstanding deals with the man.

"Honorable Judge Hansley, we bring before you the woman responsible for the grave robbing that has been going on for the last four years." Wilhelm spoke, approaching the man in the long black robe.

"Four years?" J'ai questioned, arching a brow. "Didn't feel that long." She would shrug. "Time flies when you're having fun I suppose." Her tone was as calm as ever.

"That will be enough, miss Mauvais." Her gaze dulled as he addressed her. "I'm under the impression, given your calloused words, you seek no counsel in this accusation?" He asked her, looking down on her from his judge's bench. "Do you stand before me this day and openly admit to the crimes you are being charged with?" He leaned forward, annoyed with her silence at this point. "Speak woman!" He exclaimed.

"Firstly Your Honor, I am Madam J'ai Francisca Mauvais, my family has lived in this city far longer than any of you rats have been. I will be addressed in a manner befitting my title, however sullied it may be at this point." She would step forward then. "However, to answer your question, no, I will not defend myself against these accusations. I was caught red handed, not only by another Inspector, whom I killed without hesitation, but by the young brat who pissed himself as he watched." Wilhelm snapped to attention at that last statement.

"How do you know about our witness?!" He exclaimed in

that moment.

"Oh please, even a deaf man could hear his blubbering from three gravestones away." She smirked then. "Though you openly telling me just solidified my suspicions, really Willy you should be more careful. Next time it could be a bluff, not all criminals are as observant as I am." He was clearly shaken in that moment. "Had I been a colder person I'd have killed the boy as well, but killing children is not something that interests me. Killing in general doesn't – too dirty, too hard to get the stains out of clothes." She added, turning her dry gaze back to the judge.

"In all my years on this bench I've never seen such a cold display. Even men have stood where you are now, crying and blubbering for mercy." He shook his head. "You are a true monster, Madam." She smirked at the last statement. "Do you feel no remorse for the pain and suffering you've caused to the family members of the deceased?" He asked, staring down at her intently.

"Of course not." She answered simply. "Why feel sorry for those that are already dead?" The judge even looked shocked this time. "I was harming no one, what was once human was nothing more than a rotting corpse left in the soil. They still had their uses, knowledge worth studying in the name of medical science." She said, her tone matter-of-fact as she spoke. "How is it any different than what most medical students do, hm?" She asked, keeping her eyes locked onto the judge. "How is what I've done any worse than what they do to the unwanted corpses of prisoners and war criminals? It's discrimination, really." He slammed the gavel on his bench and stood abruptly.

"That will be quite enough, Madam Mauvais!" He exclaimed. "It is clear to me you harbor no guilt for your actions. You've desecrated the graves of many families, defiled their memories and left what was left of their relatives in shame and sorrow, and you murdered a protector of this city in cold blood. Crimes like these are serious, and even in light of that you show no fear as it is clear you know too well what awaits you." He slammed the gavel down again. "By the power invested in me by our Queen, I sentence you to be hanged by the neck until dead." He sat back down. "May God have mercy on your soul." He added.

"May he indeed." She said with a cold grin as she was escorted back out.

She didn't know how much time passed, she didn't pay attention. Days, weeks, months? It felt like a blink, though maybe some would say it felt like an eternity, but then again she had an eternity to figure out what a true one felt like. Again she heard the door crash open, the clink, the hobbled walk, of course he would be there for this. She smirked and slowly stood up, she had been stripped of her normal attire and forced to wear the garb meant for the female prisoners, though there weren't many of them. Seemed not many women committed worthy enough crimes to warrant the death penalty. She was already waiting at the cell doors, hands poking out awaiting the shackles, Wilhelm's steps slowed as he noticed this and his eyes slowly drifted up to her.

"Were you expecting a struggle?" She asked, tilting her head slightly.

"Honestly?" He asked, and her head craned to the opposite side. "I don't know what to expect from you anymore." Her head straightened out as the shackles went around her wrists. "Nothing about you could ever surprise me again." He added, opening the cell door.

"Well then." She chuckled as she stepped past him. "Stick around, and come back to me with that at the end of the day." His brows furrowed at that, clear confusion.

She walked with confidence as they approached her end, she assumed it would be a spectacle. She wondered if Louis would be there – likely not, but she still wondered. She watched the empty streets pass by once they were in the carriage, Wilhelm seemed more concerned than she did. Perhaps it was her lack of concern that set him on edge, or maybe he was still thinking on what she'd said to him. It was amusing to watch him think, she was eager to see the look he would have afterwards. It wouldn't be long now. She was taken from the carriage and marched up to the gallows, it seemed like they put it together just for her.

The rope was placed around her neck, and as she felt it tighten around her throat she stared back to the crowd who looked upon her with disgust. She couldn't stop smiling. "Lady J'ai Francisca Mauvais, you have been sentenced to death by hanging. Before your life is ended, is there anything left you'd like to say to the family of the victims?" The man at the front of the stage asked.

"They were already dead, there were no victims." She said simply.

"You're a monster." Her eyes flicked to the voice, those blonde curls resting on her shoulders still, she could see her eyes this time. Green. "You...defiled my brother. Pulled him from his place of rest and tortured his corpse!" Her voice cracked.

"Little girl, you can't torture a corpse." She grinned wide. "I can show you true torture, if you'd like." She saw the shiver visibly travel down the girl's spine.

"As ordered by our Queen, and this country we love so, you will now be hanged by the neck until death. May God have mercy on your soul." The man spoke, and then looked to the other waiting for the signal to pull the switch.

She felt the floor fall away from her, it was a fantastic, liberating feeling. The way the spectators slowly floated up, and then the sudden, taught stop. The sound, the crack of her neck and pushing of her larynx, it was so sudden. It was just like when she'd decapitated herself, well, almost, minus the head coming off. This time she only lost consciousness for a few seconds, and that... that was the best part of all. The collective gasp of the crowd as her eyes slowly opened up once more, the grin that stretched over her face as hands lifted to their mouths.

"Well, that was fun!" She craned her neck to look up to the executioner and announcer. "You two just going to stand there? Pull me back up!" She cackled as she hung there. "Willy!" She found his shocked face in the crowd. "Give us a hand, no point in just hanging around now is there?" She laughed, knowing now they had no choice.

Chapter Two

Fire burns – I never thought to test that – burning myself alive. I think fire brings me the closest to death – it lasts about five minutes more than the hanging, and the beheading, and both last even less than drowning. I'm learning a lot with these fools – what methods might work best given enough time and persistence. I wonder what they have in store for me today… I'm excited to find out.

It had been several months – she didn't bother counting the days – she simply wondered when they would give up. She also wondered what they would decide to do with her in the end, once they finally came to the conclusion that death was not so easy for her. Even the executioner and all his skills of torture were no match for her – she heard he quit after she laughed at him after coming out of the iron maiden. The Queen was likely beside herself – she could only imagine the fat hag pacing about her lavish bedroom, not at all amused by her own servants' failure to kill a simple prisoner, but then it wasn't so simple was it, and the torturers nor the executioner could be held to blame. After all, it was her own greed that made her this way.

"Time to eat." She slowly looked to the sound of Wilhelm's voice, a hollow smile painted on her lips as she stood. Her hair was short, likely burned away in the pyre, but she knew it would grow back with time.

"Not even going to indulge a bit of conversation with me, Willy?" She asked, taking the metal tray he'd offered her. "What, no pudding?" She asked dryly, staring at the stale slice of bread and spoiled meat stew she was offered.

"Stop calling me that." He growled through grit teeth.

She eyed him then. "What, Willy? I always called you Willy."

She said, in a tone that was more like she was still a free woman.

"When we were children...when we were *friends*!" He turned to face her once more – then his expression softened when he looked into her eyes. A shuddered sigh passed his lips. "Why... how are you like this?" He asked, gripping the bars.

Her coy smirk had all but faded – she looked at him now with emotionless eyes. The eyes of a dead woman. "Greed." She answered simply. "To have something I didn't believe I could ever have otherwise." She turned and sat on her cot, lightly picking at the food offered to her.

"Greed... to live forever? How did you do it?" He asked leaning in closer.

"I don't remember. It all happened so quickly." She looked up to the small barred window that offered a faint glow of light – the only way she could tell if it was night or day any more. "There was a fire – I was trapped in the room... Louis came to find me and then..." She smirked and turned her eyes back to Wilhelm. "Looking to live forever, Willy?" She asked, her grin spreading.

"No." He replied without hesitation – which caused her eyes to widen slightly. "What you have is not a blessing – it is a curse... a disease." Her smile softened as he spoke, and for a moment he saw the girl he used to know.

"I'm glad you can see it for what it is." She would say, and then she took in a deep breath. "How will Her Majesty try to kill me today, Wilhelm?" She asked, looking at him from the corner of her eye.

"I've heard nothing today... been quiet since last time." He said, unable to keep a lock onto her gaze.

"Maybe they've finally given up." She brought a spoonful of bile to her mouth, and grimaced at the taste. "How I miss Lou-Lou's fine cooking." She sighed softly.

"Her Majesty doesn't give up. She only grows more clever, and I'm sure she will come up with something." He blinked when she started to laugh wildly.

"Clever?" She laughed out once more as the word left her own lips. "That old cow is anything but clever!" She added, nearly unable to contain herself.

"How dare you speak of our Queen in such a manner!" He barked but froze when the metal door at the end of the hall opened.

A man dressed in a white suit slowly walked down the stone hallway, his hands clasped behind his back as he approached Wilhelm. He had the Queen's mark on his lapel, and the moment Wilhelm saw it he quickly bowed at the waist, but the man paid no attention to the Inspector and instead turned immediately to look at J'ai. They had the same, bored gaze as they looked at one another, until finally he turned his head back to Wilhelm who finally stood up straight.

"I am Her Majesty's Royal Hand, she sent me here with a letter for you, Inspector Goddard." He said, extending the envelope with the Queen's seal out to him, his eyes finally looking towards Goddard's. "To simplify matters, you've been relieved of your duties here, you can return to your place at Prim from this moment on." Wilhelm looked at the other man in shock.

"Relieved...of my duties?" He questioned softly. "...Why?" He asked then, not even bothering to open the letter.

"Because Her Majesty has decided that if the prisoner

cannot be killed either by hanging, fire, or firing squad, then there is not much left to do in the matter." He stated. "However, that does not mean Miss Mauvais gets to simply walk out of custody or out of the Queen's ever watchful eyes, no." He turned his gaze back to J'ai then. "J'ai...Continental origin I believe, yes?" He asked, tilting his head slightly.

"My mother was from the Continental Republic, yes, but my father was born and raised here in Great Victoria as a noblewoman. Just as I was raised, and as he grew into a man of science as did I become a woman seeking knowledge." She replied, crossing her arms slowly.

The man smirked. "I've come with a message for you as well, Madam Mauvais. From this day forward you are hereby labeled a criminal of the highest order, and it has come to Her Majesty's attention that you cannot be simply put to death. So she has decided you will be freed."

"What?!" Both Wilhelm and J'ai spoke suddenly.

"Please, allow me to finish." He said, but Wilhelm stepped forward with clenched fists.

"You said she wouldn't simply be able to walk out of here!" He bellowed.

"If you would let me finish, sir, you'll find it isn't so simple." He stated, glaring down at the other man. "Her Majesty, herself pained by the suffering you caused to her people, has decided that instead of the usual punishments you will work for her and for the people of Great Victoria. The people you have wronged." He stated coldly.

"Excuse me?" J'ai asked with a raised brow. "The people of Great Victoria want nothing from me, and I can do nothing for them." She said, waving her hand idly.

"No?" He chuckled softly. "You, Madam, are the perfect pawn to be at Her Majesty's disposal. You fear no death, as death will never come for you. Not to mention the extensive training you likely received from your father in the medical field, as well as the field of science. You have much to contribute to this fine country for as long as the royal bloodline remains and for as long as you live… as wretched as a life it may be." He smirked as he eyed her. "Either that or you are left to spend however long is necessary in this cell, deep underground the Victorian city." He added, watching her carefully.

There was a long moment of silence that filled the room. The eyes of the Queen's royal lap dogs and her own remained locked for what seemed like forever, until J'ai finally scoffed and stood from her cot. "Fetch my butler, Louis. Have him bring me a change of clothes and some real food." She stated, crossing her arms over her chest once more.

"So you agree?" The man dressed in white asked.

"What choice do I have?" She asked, giving a cold smirk. "Truly this isn't at all what I expected." She added with a light chuckle. "Saves the hassle of killing everyone and walking out of here, either way I get to walk out, this just requires less dirty work." Her grin grew across her lips, and Wilhelm merely watched and wondered how she'd become like this.

"Victoria's Monster. The Queen's loyal beast." He placed a gloved hand over his chest and gave a slight bow. "My name is Simon Cordel, you and I will be seeing a lot of one another from this day on…" His own smirk grew. "Madam Mauvais."

A bittersweet freedom, out of one cell and figuratively into another. The cell door remained open and Wilhelm, despite being given his leave, remained outside the door at the end of the hallway. Louis had arrived the moment he was summoned and now he stood in her cell, carefully buttoning her shirt for her before slowly kneeling down and placing her shoes upon her feet. She sat silent, the both of them knowing without words that speaking was not the best idea in a place like this. Not with the Queen's lap dog idling about. It wasn't long before she and Louis were walking down that hallway, and out the door, greeted with a glare from Wilhelm as they passed.

"I loved you like family." She would pause, and only a moment after Louis would pause as well, glancing back at her just as she turned to face Wilhelm for that moment. "I...always thought..."

"What?" She asked in a cold tone. "That perhaps one day we would be lovers? That I would marry you and bear your children?" This caused Wilhelm a small choke in his throat. "Is that it, am I right?" She tilted her head slightly.

"...J'ai." He said her name softly.

"You should have known from the start that I could never love someone like you." Louis looked at her, he was unshaken by her cold words. In a way admiring her as she stripped away any past hopes the Inspector might have had, and any he may have remaining. "Perhaps at one point I loved you as well, but never more than one loves the household dog. You amused me, with your idle dreams and chatter of making this city great, even after we grew up I knew you still had your uses." She turned her back to him, continuing to walk. "That's all you ever were Willy, a tool at my disposal." Wilhelm's hands trembled as she walked away. "Come, Louis."

"Yes, Madam." He answered, and quietly followed her.

She took in a deep breath as they stepped out into the city air, people passing by staring at her, confused, knowing full well who and what she was, but she didn't care. Louis wasted no time opening the carriage door for her, and helped her inside before quickly joining her. The sound of hooves on cobblestone was one that she didn't realize she missed until now. She was safe, and free of that tiny cell with the foul food. She leaned back in her seat, arms crossed over her chest as she watched the houses and shops pass out the window on their way back to the manor. Her brows furrowed as her mind wandered back to Simon's words, and the more she thought on it the more it annoyed her.

"The Queen's Loyal Beast." Her eyes snapped to Louis, who stared right back at her with a dry gaze. "It has a bit of a ring to it, don't you think?"

"I'm hardly loyal to that old cow." She stated, her lip curling in annoyance.

"It's funny, because you called Sir Wilhelm a tool. A house pet." He smiled lightly, though his humor was macabre at best. "Yet now, it seems, you've become the house pet, Madam." His eyes shifted to her, a cold emerald gaze.

"I'm glad you find this humorous." She stated, leaning back in her seat and resigning herself to staring out the window.

"Humorous?" He chuckled then. "I find it ironic, and nothing is more amusing than a bit of irony Madam." He added, resting his chin upon the ball of his hand. "Will you obey?" He asked quietly.

She was silent for a moment as she weighed her options. "For now." She would answer after a moment. "I suppose this is better than wasting my brain away in that dull little cell with their slop they feed to us." She scoffed, closing her eyes then.

"What of your experiments? Will you continue to gather subjects?" He blinked slowly as he watched her open her eyes to stare at the roof of the carriage.

"In time. This was merely an inconvenience." She would lean forward then. "If I were to start right back up where I left off, it would be rather obvious. I'll need to find a new site to gather subjects from, perhaps a small town where no one knows me or the happenings in the city. Though a small break won't hurt, in the meantime you can gather information on some new promising locations for when we begin again." She said, eyeing him then.

"So you've no intention of giving up?" His expression never changed.

"No. You should know by now, my dear Lou-Lou, I don't give up." She leaned forward, practically sitting in his lap as her hands cradled either side of his face. "I only get more persistent." A smirk spread across her lips and he returned it with one of his own.

"Yes, that's the woman I'm proud to serve." He replied, allowing her to enjoy herself in that moment. "I won't lie, it's been too quiet around the manor since you've been gone."

Chapter Three

"Louis!"

Her voice rang out from her bedroom, a clear annoyance in her tone. The sound of her footsteps stomping down the hall growing ever closer. She slammed the door open, her hand remaining on the door as she glared at the male before her. His expression, while dull usually, showed slight confusion as she approached and slapped him sharply across the face. He would remain still, practically unfazed by her harshness in that moment, but slowly his head craned back to look down at her. His emerald hues locked with the dark hazel that glared back into his.

"I was gone for only four months! What the hell is this!?" She asked, tossing a curtain down on the floor in front of them. "Blue?!" She exclaimed. "You know I *hate* the color blue." His eyes shifted to the curtain on the floor.

"Odd, I don't remember putting that up." He said kneeling down and picking it up. "Where was this?" He asked as he stared at the fabric, but then he hummed softly. "I certainly didn't put this up, it's far too shabby compared to anything I'd have requested." He added, turning his eyes to her.

"It was in my office. Right there behind my desk, how could you not have noticed?" She asked, crossing her arms.

"I've not been in your office since the day you left, Madam. I did as you instructed, kept an eye on where they were holding you. After all, the day I was summoned to pick you up was about a week away from when I was to free you by any means." He would place a hand over his chest and bow slightly. "Just as the letter you left behind instructed."

She scoffed. "Then who has been taking care of the manor?" She asked, glaring at him.

"Well, Madam, that would be...Caroline." He answered, taking a moment to remember her name.

"Caroline?" She questioned furrowing her brows, her lip beginning to tremble. "Stupid girl." She grumbled before stepping to the doorway once more. "Caroline!!" She exclaimed, her voice carrying like a shrill bird's.

Soft, quick footsteps were heard as a young woman came jogging down the hallway. Short red hair against porcelain skin bobbed with each movement. She seemed worried as she came to a slow stop, looking between J'ai and then to Louis before glancing down to her own trembling hands. She had a spot of dirt on her cheek, her hands were trembling. She gasped when she noticed the curtain in Louis' hand and she swallowed back a lump that had lodged itself in her throat as she slowly looked to her lady's expectant gaze.

"Yes Madam?" She asked in a soft, shaky tone.

"Did you put these curtains up in my office?" She asked, maintaining that cold glare with the younger woman.

"I did...Madam." She answered honestly.

"Why?" Jai asked, stepping closer.

"...I just thought...a bit of color would be nice for when you came home." She said, unable to maintain the gaze.

There was a long moment where J'ai just stared at the woman for a moment, her gaze softening but only slightly. It was an odd concept, someone trying to do something nice for her and that pulled a long sigh from within her before she turned back to Louis and grabbed the curtain from his hand, and rudely pushed it into Caroline's chest. The woman quickly gripped the fabric and slowly looked up to J'ai as though she expected to be hit or punished in some way.

"These suit your room more than my office. You should know I hate the color blue." She said, taking that moment to note the blue-green color of the woman's eyes. She must have noticed, as she quickly looked away.

"Am I...allowed to continue with my daily tasks now, Madam?" She asked, keeping her eyes locked onto the floor.

"Go." J'ai said quickly. "Be sure to take the other curtains down from my office before the end of the day." She added, and with that young Caroline bowed her head and quickly made her way out of the room.

Louis watched the girl go and then turned his gaze to J'ai as she sighed and rubbed her temple. "Shall I punish her, Madam?" He asked, and watched her eyes flick quickly to him.

"No." She answered in a simple tone. "She meant no harm, she was just trying to be nice." She said, heaving another sigh. There was a long moment of silence as the two stood idly in the kitchen, the kettle on the stove began to scream in the moment. "I'm not one for apologies normally but I hope you can forgive my harshness earlier." She said, watching as he removed the kettle from the stovetop.

"Of course, Madam. I, most of all, understand your hatred for the color." A smile spread over his lips. "It brings out the worst in you." He added, and continued to speak with his back pointed at her. "I'm surprised you were so understanding with young Caroline." His words hit her, and that hazel gaze flicked to the empty doorway.

"What kind of noble would I be if I whipped my servants. I acted harshly with you, without thinking, my actions were uncalled for. Believe me when I say that I did want to hit her the moment she admitted it was her, but-"

"But?" He questioned as he turned to her, he chuckled as he watched her. "Perhaps your time behind bars has made you soft in the heart, perhaps your final words to Inspector Goddard were truly a front." Her eyes snapped to him.

"Don't make me slap you again, Louis." She said dryly.

"Speaking of that day, the Queen's loyal dog delivered a letter for you today." He produced the envelope from his pocket and extended it out to her. "I intended to bring it to your office along with your morning tea but you came to me." He always had a smile, but her eyes lingered on the red of his cheek. "He insisted on seeing you himself, but I insisted more forcefully that he shouldn't." He said with a light chuckle.

She snatched the letter from his hand, and in that moment he turned and quietly began to pour the tea into a single cup for her. Her eyes scanned over the letter quickly, her eyes narrowing the more she read. "This is interesting." She muttered softly.

"What is interesting?" Louis asked as he placed the cup of tea next to her.

"Apparently there have been disappearances in this city, they started around the time I was taken into custody and grew more and more prevalent during my stay." She smirked slightly. "Men going missing in the middle of the night near the Thames, disappearing without a trace, known drunks and not a bloated body to be found washed ashore. Like they never existed." She tossed the letter down and picked up the cup, taking a slow sip from it.

"That is a bit interesting." Louis stated, picking the letter up for himself.

"Yes, but that isn't the part that interests me." She stated, her coy smirk only growing. "The bodies have started turning up. The first on the day that I was released, and this morning." She turned her eyes to Louis. "Not just one however, all of them." Louis turned his eyes up to her then. "It doesn't give more detail than that, but it is enough to peak my curiosity." Louis then tossed the letter aside.

"There was one more thing that Mr. Cordel wanted me to give you." From his pocket he produced a small, blue velvet box. "I know your hatred for the color blue but he insisted that whatever it was remain in the box. I have no idea what it is." Her eyes narrowed and her brows furrowed as she reached out and took the wretched box.

"What else comes in something like this, Louis?" She asked as she slowly opened it to reveal a gold band, with a red emerald placed inside. "Of course it's a ring." She spoke, curling her lip as she looked at the Queen's mark engraved in the band. "I suppose this is my mark." She muttered as she turned the ring around in her fingers.

"A fine collar befitting a loyal dog." Louis stated, admiring the band himself.

She huffed and slowly placed it on her index finger. "Your other cheek appears to be in need of its own shade of red more and more, Louis." She flicked her cold gaze to him once again.

He smirked and leaned forward, offering his bare cheek to her. "If that is your desire, Madam." He stated coyly.

Again she scoffed. "Have the coach ready the carriage,

we'll be heading to the scene as soon as I finish my tea. I assume Inspector Goddard will be there, and I am to guess he knows I'll be showing up soon to take a look at this crime scene for myself." She sighed softly as she leaned against the counter, taking another sip.

"As you wish, Madam." He said, placing his hand over his chest before making his way to the door.

She didn't expect to be playing detective for the Queen, she was a woman of science, a woman with medical knowledge. She couldn't help but wonder why she would be doing the Prim Guard's work, but then she also realized that most of them were idiots. They'd not even solved the Ripper case, but then it'd been years since any more whores went missing. The more she thought about it, the more she wondered if, perhaps, there was something about the bodies that she would be able to shed light on. Drunk men falling out of existence, each one kidnapped days after one another, all in the span of four months. A lot of work for a singular person, even she had to space out digging up corpses from graves – too many at once drew too much attention – and even after people started to notice the missing corpses and empty coffins, it took them several months still to figure out it was her. It wouldn't be a mistake she would repeat.

"How do you do it?" She asked herself quietly. "What are you trying to accomplish?" She took another long sip from her cup, her eyes fixated on the wall in front of her. "I do look forward to seeing your work though, whoever you are." She smirked to herself once the words fully left her lips.

The ride to the crime scene was dull, both Louis and J'ai remained silent the entire way, but inside J'ai continued to wonder about these missing men. Why drunk men? Why men in general? Was this somehow connected to her own arrest? These were questions she genuinely wanted to know the answers to. It had been a very long time since she'd been excited about anything, and somehow, as they finally came to a stop, she found herself smiling. A genuine smile out of genuine excitement. Louis stepped out first, holding his hand to the side as J'ai stepped down to the street herself. She fixed her jacket and adjusted her sleeves, before turning towards the constables that guarded the cramped alley where she could only assume the body was. A crowd of people had gathered and were trying to get a look for themselves, but moved when they saw her step forward.

"You're quite famous, Madam." Louis said softly with a grin.

"Lovely." J'ai replied as she walked up to the constables.

"This is a crime scene, please back away." One said, glaring down at her. "Or have you come to claim this body as well?" He asked, his jab made out of annoyance for her release.

"You should be careful with how you talk to me." She said before flashing the ring on her finger. "The Queen herself instructed me to come here, I need to see the body." She smirked at the shocked look on both constables' faces. "Now excuse me while I do what I was instructed." She added pushing past them, finding only enjoyment when they scoffed as she passed.

The alley was dark, even in the day, the walls on either side, and the ground stained with filth of varying degrees. The smell was also something to be desired, but truly she had still smelled worse, but one scent in particular she recognized. The familiar scent of a corpse, rotting away in the damp warmth of the alley. As she expected Wilhelm was here, and as he noticed her and Louis approaching she noted the visible annoyance in his eyes as he slowly approached them. He put a hand out to stop her and in that moment she chose to stand there as he placed his note book into his pocket and then eyed her for a moment before his gaze turned up to Louis.

"This is a crime scene, what are you two doing here?" He asked, crossing his arms over his chest.

"I'm surprised you don't know." Louis said, producing the letter from his breast pocket. "Her Majesty asked Madam Mauvais to come here and help with the investigation. So of course, we are here to look at the body." He explained, and like the contables Wilhelm scoffed.

"This is no place for a noblewoman." He said, taking his gold gaze to Louis.

"Oh please." J'ai said suddenly. "Neither is a graveyard, and yet there I was digging up corpses." She pushed past him. "Don't start trying to protect me, Inspector. I don't need it." She stated coldly.

Louis smirked down to Wilhelm and slowly stepped past him as well, the two making their way to the body covered with the white sheet. The other officers taking notes slowly moved off to the side as she stood over the covered corpse. She looked to Louis and motioned with her hand for him to uncover the body, and with a confirming nod he knelt down and peeled the sheet back. The constables and even Wilhelm couldn't stand to look at the corpse, but J'ai didn't flinch and Louis merely arched a curious brow. The body was displayed in a way that told J'ai that whoever placed it here went to a lot of trouble to make sure it was perfectly displayed. Like a piece of art for all to see, but what was most interesting was the corpse itself. Finely dressed in the nicest suit, expensive by the feel of the fabric, make-up to give the skin the color of life but it was clear that this body had long been dead, though somehow finely preserved up until it was dropped off.

"It appears the body was stitched together." Louis said softly. "A fine stitching at that." He added, kneeling down next to J'ai then.

"Indeed." J'ai replied as she ran her fingers over the stitching along the face, then neck. "This body was pieced together with a loving hand. Whoever did this put a lot of time and care into the craft. There isn't a seam out of place." She smirked softly. "The craftsmanship is beyond that of even Doctor Frankenstein, perhaps our Doll-maker took some inspiration from the famous story." She said looking to Louis then.

"Doll-maker?" Louis asked then. "Giving pet names already are we, Madam?" He added to the question.

"It's suitable I think, now that I've seen it. It also makes sense as to why the letter would say that all the bodies turned up at once. A piece of every one of the men is right here, perfectly sewn together by a careful hand." She leaned in and unbuttoned the suit, opening it to show the chest of the body and like the face and neck, there were a mixture of parts sewn together. "Like a patchwork doll." She said with a soft smile, gently running her fingers over the stitching. "This just gets more and more interesting." She muttered softly, her eyes admiring the body before her, after all a woman like her could appreciate this sort of craftsmanship.

"Why do you think this Doll-maker went to such trouble?" Louis asked as he searched the pockets of the body.

"Only the artist knows what their art means, Louis. Perhaps they were lonely and wanted to build a family." She chuckled then as she slowly stood. "Or perhaps they were simply bored." She shrugged then. "No one will know until we speak to the maker themselves." She would turn and motion to Wilhelm then. "Take this doll to the morgue. I would like to take this one apart myself, stitch by stitch." She stated, but didn't give Wilhelm time to protest. "I will be sure to examine every inch, and every detail, as the Queen instructed me. Not only that but I doubt your bumbling idiot of a doctor would be as gentle as the one that put this doll together to begin with. I can't have some hack carving away at a masterpiece." She said, crossing her arms over her chest.

"You sound like you admire this monster." Wilhelm said, glaring at her. "Like you appreciate this level of butchery." He added, staring at her with disgust.

"Even monsters can appreciate the works of other monsters." She said with a simple grin. "Get this body back to the Prim, I'll be along shortly to examine. If the outside is patched together like this, I'm curious to see what the Doll-maker did with the insides." She turned away then, both her and Louis heading back out to the carriage.

She stepped inside with a smile painted on her lips, her eyes staring out the window as Louis seated himself in front of her. "You seem happy, Madam." He said then, causing her to turn that gaze to him. "It's good to see you looking lively again." He added with a smile of his own.

"I didn't expect to get something so interesting from the Queen. I simply assumed I'd be doing dirty work." She stated, crossing one leg over the other.

"Some would consider this dirty." He said with a chuckle.

"You know me better than that, dear Lou-Lou. This isn't dirty." She would turn her gaze out the window once more. "This is art."

As the carriage slowly pulled away the crowd remained,

watching as the bullies prepared to move the body, but a pair of dark eyes watched the carriage that had already pulled away. A tired gaze, the gaze of a man that was usually filled with boredom but now he looked on with a sense of admiration. He'd never encountered a woman that didn't shy from death, a woman that admired true art in its finest form. The crowd began to disperse as the body was loaded into a carriage of its own. He walked away, annoyed with how careless they were being with his doll, but it wasn't at all perfect. No, perfection had yet to come, but it seemed he had an admirer, he could tell. From what he saw from his place in the crowd, she had the same look in her eyes that he had while working on the doll.

"Excuse me, Inspector." He approached Wilhelm, and then pointed in the direction J'ai's carriage had gone. "Who was that strange woman?" He asked, crossing his arms.

"You don't know?" Wilhelm said with an arched brow.

"She seems familiar, but I've not been in Great Victoria for very long. I just returned from holiday." He said, producing a card from his own breast pocket. "My name is Henry Blithe, I'm a furniture maker and also deal in repairs." He added as Wilhelm took the card.

"On holiday, eh? I hope it was nice, I'm sorry you had to return to such a vile scene." Wilhelm sighed then. "As for that woman...that was J'ai Mauvais, and her butler, Louis Cartwright. She's...rather infamous around the city these days." He added, shaking his head softly.

"That odd woman I've read about in the papers? The grave robber?" He asked, and his eyes widened as he turned his gaze in the direction her carriage had gone. "Interesting that Her Majesty would allow her near the dead, or freedom for that matter." He said, rubbing the stubble on his chin gently.

"You must have been away for a while to not know any of the circumstances." Wilhelm pointed out, a brow arching in confusion.

"I don't really read the papers, I simply glance at the headlines. I'm afraid I don't know much of the goings-on these days." He chuckled lightly. "Well, if you'll excuse me, I should get back to my store. Thank you for indulging my curiosity Inspector, and I'm sorry if I wasted any of your time." He added with a slight bow before heading off down the sidewalk.

Wilhelm watched the strange man go, and made a mental note of him. He was well dressed, a black suit with a gray button down shirt. His hands, from the look of them now, were rough, perhaps from his own crafting work, but it was still odd that he had so many questions about J'ai rather than the crime that had been committed, and he didn't at all seem shocked by the incident itself. He climbed into the carriage and took his notebook from his pocket and placed the man's card into the page before writing below it. He would make a note to visit this shop, Henry's Comfort Design and Repair, and then closed the book before rubbing his own chin thoughtfully.

A killer wouldn't visit their own crime scene...would they?

Chapter Four

The store was silent, furniture on display sat quietly in the dimly lit room. The sign on the door was set to close, and all was silent within the shop, all was as it should be. Distant footsteps grew closer and the door opened with a soft click, and the gentle tone of the bell above. Henry would take in a breath and once more lock the door, keeping the sign turned to closed and finally removing his jacket. He would hang it near the door, and slowly roll the sleeves of his button down up his arm as he walked behind the counter and towards the middle shelf that housed some books at the very top, a cabinet taking up the majority of the center.

He unlocked the cabinet to reveal a staircase that led down to the basement of the shop, his truth, his sanctuary. Closing the doors behind him he would descend, his footsteps echoing against the stone as he entered this place of pure beauty. The air was thick with the scent of blood, fear, and merciful words that had long since faded. The room resembled that of a morgue, the scents of various chemicals, the tables with assorted medical devices, supplies and books laid about on display. A shelf on the far wall with handcrafted glass jars with clear yellow liquid within, and within that liquid were perfectly preserved hearts.

Approaching the easternmost side of the room and gently caressing a series of drawers that lined the walls, steel cold as ice to the touch, custom built for his beautifully dirty little secret. His hand stopped on the center most drawer, and gently he unlocked it and opened the small door, gripping the metal table within and pulling it out to reveal the body of a young man, about the same age as he. His skin was a dull blue, lips shaded with the tint of death and eyes open upward to stare back into his own loving gaze. He caressed the young man's cheek and gently brushed his hair away from his eyes. A purity frozen in time, a beauty he could only hope to replicate.

"Good morning, my love." Henry whispered softly. "I did as you asked of me." He knelt down, crossing his arms on the cold metal table, resting his head upon his arms as he admired the dead man before him. "You said I should share my art with the world, and I have done just that. I've taken something hideous and made it pure and perfect, and soon enough all of Great Victoria will come to appreciate the beauty I offer to them all." He smiled, leaning his head up and reaching out with his hand to caress the corpse's cheek once more, leaning down he would dare to place a kiss on the dead man's lips.

"Help! Please anyone, help me!!" He was disturbed, and the sweet gaze of his eyes darkened.

Pounding resonated from one of the drawers next to the one opened now, and with a calming sigh he slowly pushed the body of his love back inside. "Wait a moment, my love, I'll be only a moment." He assured the corpse before gently closing the door. His glare turned to the drawer where the sounds echoed from and without care he pulled it open. "Dolls don't speak." He said in a cold tone to the man looking back at him.

Frozen locks of hair dangled before tired and weak eyes, the man trembled from the cold, or fear, or perhaps even both in that moment. He was bound in a tight, black bag up to his neck, unable to move within its confines. He tried to stammer out words of plea but Henry simply gripped the metal slab he rested on and pulled him out, leaving him for only a moment as he moved to grab a gurney and wheeled it over beside the slab. The man's frozen and shaken words fell on deaf ears as he was moved from one slab to another, left trapped in the bag as he was pushed beneath a blinding light.

"Please, sir, I've a wife and two sons!" The man pleaded, hoping the word of his family would move the other. "Please don't cut me again!" He cried, tears spilling down his face as he watched the other clatter about on a nearby tray. "I'm begging yo-"

"Tut, tut, now." Henry spoke as he pushed a smaller table near the other, instruments for sewing placed carefully across the surface. "Dolls don't speak, they sit in their silent beauty made only for the world to observe and appreciate." He said, gently touching the man's cheek. "Don't worry though, I won't cut you today. It would be too soon, besides I haven't found the perfect parts for you yet." He smiled as the man began to sob. "Don't you want to be perfect for your family? Can't you see I'm building you into something more than what you already are?" He asked and then chuckled, not giving the man time to blubber out an answer. "Dolls don't speak. Now be silent, and become perfection." He leaned down and kissed the man gently on the forehead before turning to the table.

He took up the needle and meticulously threaded it with thick twine, dipping it then into a jar of alcohol to disinfect. It wouldn't be perfect if an infection were to occur before the final product was complete. Dolls don't speak, that was the mantra in his mind at that moment, and suddenly the gentle look in his eyes went rigid and cold as he gripped the man's wiggling face with his free hand. Dolls don't speak, and they don't struggle, they are to be complacent and beautiful. Displaying their perfection to the world for all to see and admire. The man let out a cry as the needle punctured through his bottom lip, and then the top, over and over again for what felt like an eternity of agony, until the cries became muffled. The distinct snip of scissors filtered through both men's ears as the thread was perfectly cut—his mouth sewn meticulously shut.

"I promise, I will make you perfect." He smiled, brushing his thumb just beneath the man's bottom lip. "I will present you to your family, a new man. The man they deserve—the husband you could never be as you are now, the father your sons can be proud of. Perfection as a gift for those you love and who love you most of all." He leaned back, and admired his own work, the tears streaming down the other's face lost to him in that moment. "This is my gift to you." He added, and finally reached out to unfasten the leather bag that housed his body revealing a man with no arms and one leg missing, bandaged carefully so as to not waste what remained of him. "You helped make that other man perfect, and now I will do the same for you." He said as he leaned down and pressed his ear to the man's chest, listening to the heartbeat that, if it could, dared to pound right out of the other's chest. "Such a beautiful melody."

The skies had darkened by the time they made it to the station, thunder growled in the distant clouds as rain gently began to beat against the roof of the carriage. Louis was the first to step out into the dampened streets, an umbrella at the ready as J'ai made her way out next. She looked up at the dingy, gray brick walls of Primburogh and curled her lip in visible disgust. She hated this place, but at least she wasn't here to stay this time, and at least now Louis was with her to keep her company. She felt the cold gaze of the constables as she entered the building, Louis shaking the rain from the umbrella right on the floor without care of what anyone else thought.

"The hell's she doin' 'ere?" One of the constables whispered as she approached the desk at the front of the building.

"Has the body arrived yet?" She asked, staring at the man behind the counter.

"...You mean the stitched man?" He asked, scratching beneath his cap.

"No, the sodomized leprechaun." She rolled her eyes. "Yes the stitched man you idiot." She crossed her arms as she eyed the other.

"I think Inspector Goddard and Doctor Roxwell are already down in the morgue lookin' at it." He said rubbing his chin slowly.

"I told him to wait." She muttered as she turned towards one of the doors. "It's this way isn't it?" She asked as she continued down the hall.

"Wait, miss, you can't just-" He was cut off by Louis' hand in his face.

"The Madam is helping with this investigation. Directions would be helpful, good sir." He added with a kind, yet patronizing smile.

"...Aye, it's down that hall, third door on the right, stairs lead right down into it." He huffed and eyed his fellow constables who only glared at him.

She and Louis traversed the hallway, opening the door and heading down into the cool space that was the morgue. The chill didn't bother her, it only reminded her of her own work space in the manor; the cold was good for the bodies, keeping them preserved well while she studied and worked with each one. The smell wasn't much different either, the scent of formaldehyde and a vague smell of other chemicals and cleansers. Oddly it brought a smirk to her face as she pushed the double doors open, and saw Wilhelm and the mortician standing over the body. The doctor was old, with thick, round spectacles resting at the tip of his nose.

"Who are these two then, Inspector?" He asked, keeping his gaze on J'ai and Louis.

"These are the two I said would be performing the autopsy Gerald." He answered and the man hummed in acknowledgment, slowly nodding his head.

"You two don't make a mess now." He said, placing the clipboard down on the edge of the exam table. "I'll be taking an early lunch today. The wife made biscuits and homemade jam." He said slowly walking out of the room past her and Louis. "Have fun." He said, closing the doors behind him.

"...Nice fellow." J'ai said, turning her eyes back to Wilhelm then.

"He's...due for retirement." Wilhelm cleared his throat then. "However, yes, he is a nice man. A bit strange but..." He trailed off with a shrug as he turned back to the body before him.

"Strange comes required for a job like this." Louis stated as the two moved to stand near Wilhelm.

"Yes..." Wilhelm agreed, though it seemed to pain him to do so. "We did as you asked, the body wasn't touched." He stated, folding his arms over his chest.

J'ai didn't respond, she simply leaned down to get a closer look at the stitching on the arms, and around the neck. Her gaze changed as she seemingly admired the stitching, her hand raising to gently glide over each thread before she would straighten up and look around for tools. She pointed to the far table with the instruments needed, and Louis nodded as he moved to fetch them. Once the tray was next to her she took a pair of small surgical scissors in her hand

and carefully cut a portion of the stitching away, tugging it from the dead flesh and then twirling it in her fingertips. Her brows furrowed as she examined it, her head tilting ever so slightly.

"This isn't any type of stitching a doctor would use, it's a bit too thick." She said, rolling the thread between her index and thumb to force it to fray. "This is a fine thread used for stitching fabric." She added, and then Louis would lean in to look.

"Perhaps Doll-maker was an apt nickname after all, Madam." He said, keeping his hands folded behind his back.

"It's not the right kind of thread for a doll's clothing though, still too thick. It's strong, crafted for the purpose of repairing furniture perhaps." She would hand the thread off to Louis as she moved to examine more.

He twirled the thread between his own fingers. "A fine thread indeed, soft to the touch, and with an eye for detail as this Doll-maker has I'm sure a stitch as fine as this would go unnoticed in a repaired suit, it isn't far off from the kind of thread used on adult clothing." He stated, placing it down on the table then. "A tailor perhaps? There are several shops in the area where the body was left that make and repair custom suits and dresses." He added, eyeing J'ai.

She hummed thoughtfully. "Perhaps." She answered, but it was clear she was focused now. "I need to look deeper." She murmured, taking the scalpel into her hand casually.

"Hold on, you heard Gerald, no messes." He said, locking eyes with her then.

"Please, I've dealt with corpses enough to know how to not make a mess." She said and leaned over the body, gently

39

pulling the sheet away from its chest. Once uncovered she stood back, and tilted her head before turning her eyes back to Wilhelm. "You said neither of you did anything to this body." She pointed to the stitching at the chest.

He shook his head. "We were confused too, that's how he was." He said, raising his hands defensively then. "We didn't do a thing." He added.

"Whoever this Doll-maker is has a fair amount of knowledge and skill when it comes to opening a body." She would press her ear to the dead man's stomach then, before pushing her hand against the dead flesh.

There was an odd amount of give, and once more her brows furrowed thoughtfully — there was something odd about how easily her hand pressed into the stomach with little resistance, even the dead have a bit of push-back from the organs. She was still for a moment, thoughtful, before she slowly pressed the scalpel to the stomach, just below the chest, and slowly sliced downward to the top of the navel. She cut with precision, and the whole time Wilhelm watched he felt like his own stomach was going to empty its contents. Once finished she took another tool from the tray, using it to hold the sliced flesh open. She stepped back for a moment and removed her jacket, Louis immediately taking it from her, and then rolled the sleeves of her shirt up to her elbows. It was a single motion as she reached inside the stomach and felt around with her eyes closed for a short moment before removing her hand.

"Nothing." She stated simply.

"N-nothing?" Wilhelm questioned, his eyes shocked.

"Not a thing." She chuckled then and reached back inside. "Well, nothing but sawdust anyway." She said, pulling out a handful of the tiny wood chips.

"How did this person get the organs out, and the sawdust in?" Wilhelm asked, moving to get a closer look, but only slightly.

"Probably through the opening in the chest. Stuffed it like one would stuff..." She trailed off slowly and looked back to the thread. "Furniture." She said softly, a smirk spreading over her lips. "That's clever." She chuckled.

Wilhelm's brows furrowed this time, as he remembered the strange man from the crime scene. "What do you mean by furniture?" He asked, and her eyes snapped to him.

"I thought as much when I first looked at the thread — furniture stores use a soft, but strong thread such as this." She said, tapping the space of the table beside the thread. "Furniture repair is delicate work, no one wants to sit in a chair with rough, coarse threading, and the one's responsible are likely going to take extra care to be as seamless as possible." She would shrug then. "It's only a theory, but..." She trailed off and looked to Louis then. "I'd like you to go and find out how many furniture stores are around the area of the crime scene." She said, and his hand moved to his chest as he gave a slight bow.

"It will be done, Madam." Louis answered, and moved towards the door.

"Louis..." Wilhelm spoke then, causing the man to stop and glance at him. "Could you... check for a specific store in the area?" He asked and produced his notebook, taking the card from within the pages and handing it out to Louis.

"Henry's Custom Comfort and Repair." Louis hummed thoughtfully, then looked back to Wilhelm. "Where did you get this?" He asked, locking eyes with the Inspector.

"A short, finely dressed man gave it to me as we were readying the body for transport. He asked questions about you, J'ai." He answered, turning his eyes to her then.

"Interesting. Someone in this damned city that actually doesn't know me." She looked to Louis and nodded — telling him silently it was fine to indulge Wilhelm's request.

"I will have a look, Inspector." He would turn back to J'ai then. "Are you sure you will be fine on your own, Madam?" He asked.

She waved her hand passively. "Of course, dear Lou-Lou. I'm sure Inspector Goddard would be happy to escort me wherever I need to go in your absence." She said, smirking towards Wilhelm then.

"As you wish, I will try to be quick." Louis stated, and then turned a cold gaze to Wilhelm before exiting the room.

There was a long moment of silence between the two left in the room. He watched as she took the time to sew the stomach back up, and continued to watch as she examined the skin, the arms, back as well as the legs before she moved up to the face. He would admit it was a little odd to see how calm she was in a morgue, most women found them terrifying, but given where she was not too long ago it wasn't all that surprising in the long run. He still wondered though, how did the sweet girl he used to know turn into this creature before him now? What happened, what went wrong? It still disturbed him.

"Quiet." She stated suddenly, the words caused him to jump ever so slightly.

"Excuse me?" He asked, and she glanced up at him.

"You're being oddly quiet — brooding isn't a good look for

you, Wilhelm." He scoffed at her words and crossed his arms.

"What are you looking for?" He asked, silently pouting about her attention to detail.

"Not much to find, we already know whoever did this kept the organs. Feeling around in there I reached into the chest cavity and, as suspected, the heart is gone." She would tap the dead man's cheek. "This head does not belong to this torso, the neck is far thicker than the body, clearly it belonged to a man with some weight to him. Arms are the same, as is the left leg." She sighed softly then. "All that remains of the original body is the torso and right leg." She would look to Wilhelm then. "That isn't all though, here come look." She said, motioning for him to stand next to her. "See the coloration on the skin of the arms, compared to the head and chest?" She asked, and he nodded slowly. "The coloration of the arms show's signs of excessive blood flow, which means whoever these arms and legs came from might very well still be living — or was alive at the time of their removal." His eyes widened then.

"You said there wasn't much to find." He said, turning that shocked gaze to her.

"I mean, the poor man is missing two arms and a leg, there likely isn't much left to be found, Inspector." She smirked as she side eyed him.

"You crack jokes while there is a man out there, right now, suffering!?" He exclaimed, pointing toward a window above doctor Roxwell's desk.

"The chances of survival from a dismemberment like this is unlikely. As we speak the man is, probably, dead." She shrugged then. "If not then, yes, more than likely he is in extreme pain, possibly delusional from blood loss. Best case, adrenaline is keeping him alive, maybe dulling some of the pain, but I doubt he will live through another night… and if our Doll-maker has anything to say about it, he won't." She turned to Wilhelm then. "More than likely, whoever has done this is preparing him." She rubbed her chin. "Maybe he is out there right now, looking for new parts." She glanced down at the body.

"Why? Why mutilate these men like this?" He asked, shaking his head slowly.

"Perhaps this person doesn't see it as mutilation." She answered with a gentle voice. "They put a lot of time and care into this work." She looked to Wilhelm once more. "Whoever did this put as much love into the redesigning of these men as they likely do into their own day-to-day work." She chuckled then, looking to the floor. "Love." She said the word in almost a whisper.

"You think the Doll-maker did this… out of love?" He asked, staring at the body on the table.

"Love makes us do things we wouldn't normally do, Inspector." His eyes would turn to her, watching as she put her jacket on once more. "Love can be a cure, taking all the light we have within us and focusing it on a singular thing or person…" She trailed off then as her eyes darkened once more. "Love can also be a poison, making us do things we never would have done before. Love can be evil." She stated as she grabbed the sheet and tossed it over the face of the man on the table. "Love can destroy the best of us." She added, stepping past Wilhelm then.

He could only watch as she opened the door and started making her way up the stairs – there was something personal in her words, he could feel it. The girl he knew, maybe she was still in there, maybe it was love that hurt her. His eyes stayed fixated as the door slowly went shut, his shoulders slumping as the room was silent once more. His mind went back to the man on the street, and somehow it just didn't seem possible that someone who'd commit such a crime would risk returning to the scene. Could it be a coincidence? Even J'ai came to the possible conclusion that it was a furniture maker, and there he was, a man that ran a shop that crafted and repaired furniture. It was too convenient not to be suspicious.

"J'ai!" He called after her, deciding it was best to stay with her then.

She turned back to look down the stairs to see him jogging up. "What now?" She asked with a dry tone.

"You assured Louis that I would remain by your side in his absence, it would be a disservice if I were to let you go off on your own now." He said, a nerviness to his tone as he spoke.

"Fine." She said, noting Wilhelm's shock that she didn't have some snappy words to make him let her go off. "Any place around here that serves decent tea?" She asked, continuing on ahead.

Chapter Five

Louis walked along the roads that connected to the scene of the crime, the rain beat down hard on the umbrella and for a short moment he paused and dared a glance upward, allowing some of the droplets to hit his face. He'd gone to the only three stores in the area, he had learned that at one point there were four stores originally and the oldest one closed down after the owner died. Two of the stores he visited were on the verge of closing themselves, likely now more than ever since the body turned up, but it was none of those stores, at least there was nothing that pointed towards them and upon examining their craft it was clear none of them were the culprit as the stitch was something to be desired.

He stood idly for a moment, watching people walk by him slowly. He reached into his jacket and produced the card Wilhelm had given him. The address on the card pointed off the beaten path, closer to the East end of town rather than here in the city itself. The East end of town was not a well off part either, it was unlikely that this man ever got clients, and if he did it was only out of desperation or because his prices were cheap. A part of him doubted this was anything worth looking into, but he did say he would humor Wilhelm. He pocketed the card once more and waved down a taxi carriage, offering the address to the driver and spent the remainder of the ride staring out the window as they traveled.

He took in the scenery, sad looking pubs, men and women sleeping and working the streets and corners. East End was not the part of town to have a shop for furniture. He blinked and pounded on the front of the carriage for the driver to stop, and for a moment he stared at the docks in the distance. The docks where the men had originally gone missing, He'd not realized before that this area would be on the way to this particular shop. It moved a curious hum from within him, and a more confident feeling. He got the feeling that he should look around the shop first before going inside, it seemed to be the smartest thing to do given this was turning out to be a more promising lead than he originally anticipated.

"Perhaps I should explore the docks since I'm this way." He thought, eyeing the docks as he approached the front of the carriage. "I'll find my way from here on foot. Thank you, sir." He said, handing a few shillings over before watching the driver go on his way.

He walked along the docs, watching the water with a thoughtful gaze, for a moment he put himself in the mindset of the victims. Perhaps they walked this same path, all of them drunk and stumbling back towards home. He came to a stop in front of a little hole-in-the-wall pub; men were already inside indulging for the day, but then he assumed there wasn't much to do in this part of the city other than drink, or to forget. He stepped inside, and a few eyes turned to him, taking in his well fitted black suit, his finely combed black hair, and how clearly out of place he seemed visibly compared to these harder looking figures. He approached the bar, and stood by an empty stool as the pub owner gave him a look before arching a brow.

"What're ya doin' in this part o' town, sir?" He asked, raising a mug as he silently asked if Louis wanted a drink.

He shook his head. "I'm here to ask some questions. Some men from this side of town have gone missing recently." The man nodded slowly at his words.

"Aye, James Cartier, Strong-Arm Joe, and Ichabod Blithe." He shook his head solemnly then. "Ichabod was the most recent." He added, wiping the mug he'd offered before and placing it back below the counter.

"Were they regulars here?" He asked, taking a seat then.

"Aye, Ichabod was slowly becoming one, he was a sad bloke." He shook his head once more. "Poor boy was newly married, then lost his damn shipping job. Boy has a son, and had a daughter." His eyes fell to the counter sadly.

"Had?" Louis asked. "I assume there was an accident?" He added to the question.

"You're almost right, sir. Indeed it was an accident, nothing he or his wife could do, money was running short, food was hard to come by and the missus wasn't able to feed the baby on her own. No wet nurse works for free, least of all for us 'ere in the East end. Poor babe just slipped away in the night." He made a cross over his chest. "May the little lamb rest in peace." He added.

"So it's safe to say the death of his infant drove him to the bottle?" He rubbed his chin and looked around at all the eyes on him. "It's a bit obvious that you folks don't get many customers like myself?" He asked then.

"Heavens no, no one as finely dressed as you ever comes to these parts of town. Most of these blokes are fishermen, whalers, dock workers or jobless. Scraping by just enough to fill their bellies with drink and hoping for a dry night and a safe place to sleep. Why do ya ask, sir?" He questioned, leaning against the counter.

"Have you seen any strange faces walk in here on the night of the disappearances? Someone that doesn't really stand out to everyone else, but perhaps seems partially peculiar to you?" He asked, producing a notepad from his breast pocket.

"That's an odd question... well... the night Ichabod went missing, there was an odd fellow that came in. Looked a tad rough about the collar." He rubbed his chin thoughtfully. "Honestly, at first I thought nothin' of it, he looked like all the other dock workers, but then he sat with no one, he drank nothing but water, and he just kept lookin' round the room like he was waitin' for someone." He said, turning his eyes to Louis then.

"Was he still here when Ichabod left?" Louis asked then.

"Well… I dunno… I feel like I saw 'im leave a little while after Ichabod showed up. I know he wasn't there at the end of the night 'cause he left Matilda a nice tip on the table." He said, shrugging softly. "She might know more… but she hasn't been around today. Her man came back from a whaling trip and she asked for the day off." He said, shrugging once more.

"Well, I won't bother the miss on such a good day with sour conversation." Louis stated as he stood from the bar. "Thank you, sir, you've answered a lot of questions I had." He looked back to the far table the bar owner had motioned towards. "One last thing, there is a furniture store around this part of town. I was wondering how far away from here it might be?" He asked, placing his notebook back into his pocket.

"Henry's place?" He asked, and rubbed the back of his neck. "Not too far, though I have to admit I don't think he gets much business. He's a cold little fecker, I think he lives at the top of that old store too." He shook his head. "Probably lost any business he had when he and that other feckin' fairy spoke openly about their sinful relationship." He shook his head.

"Does Henry frequent this bar?" He asked, tilting his head.

"No sir. No feckin' fairies would dare step foot in this bar. I'd serve them just the same but me other customers would likely drag them out back. Like James and Joe had to that lover o' his." He leaned forward then. "You didn't hear this from me, but I heard Joe beat the poor little bastard to death, Primburogh refused to even investigate the issue because of the part of town they lived in. Told Henry that if he and his partner wanted to live that kind of life they ought to have taken the first boat to France." He shook his head. "Suppose to be a lot of their kind in France, that's what I heard anyway." He eyed Louis then.

"I see, thank you. If I have any more questions I'll be back." He bowed slightly and the bar owner nodded his head in return.

He stepped outside and turned his eyes around the street. The pub faced the water, and was rather close to the docks. Just down the way the housing developments began, and for a moment he stood there. He pictured a drunk Ichabod stumbling along the dock, heading towards home. Likely he would take an alley as a shortcut, the strange man watching him the entire night, perhaps even nights before that particular evening. Slowly he would step into a nearby alley himself, and stare down the long brick-laden hall before him, taking note of every little crack and crevice one could hide in. He imagined it was quick, a sharp pain in the back of the drunk's head, and then darkness, blanketed by a welcoming bed of cold stone.

Following the directions given to him until he came before a small shop, it stood out against the rest of the buildings. They were rundown, falling apart it seemed, while this one sat silent in its own timelessness. The store was well cared for, which told Louis that Henry did have some customers, enough to keep his shop running anyway. The sign on the door was flipped to show that it was now opened which was enough to invite Louis a look inside. The showroom was well lit, and exposed the beauty of Henry's own product. Seamless design, and heartfelt craftsmanship, each unique and intricate in their own way. He brushed a hand over one of the chairs in the center of the room, taking in the gentle fabric, the professional stitch along each of the edges.

"Welcome to Henry's Comfort Design and Repair, good sir." The voice caused Louis to turn and look at the man standing at a door to the back left of the counter.

He wore a painted smile on his face, and had bandages on his fingertips. A clear sign of someone who works with sharp things, needles were a hassle and he only assumed that the bandages covered up fresh jabs. The one they are looking for has a steady hand, too steady to likely be puncturing themselves. He smiled at Henry and turned his eyes back to the chair before him, it was a nice office chair, custom designed it seemed. High quality carpentry, intricate designs falling down the side of the chair's frame, and fitted with a delicately hand sewn cushion and backing that was attached neatly to the chair itself. His eyes flicked back to the man, and briefly to his fingers which were carefully, and freshly, bandaged. Not even a speck of blood showing through.

"You own this store?" Louis would ask suddenly, slowly approaching the counter as he looked over each piece of display furniture.

"Yes, sir, well… It was a gift from a dear friend of mine after he passed away. I've been caring for it ever since." He spoke with an honest tone, a friendly tone. "I know what you're thinking." He would add, causing Louis to take a look at him from the corner of his eye. "How does a place like this manage in this part of town?" He smirked softly and nodded his head. "Yes, just about everyone asks when they walk in here. You see, it's the glory of my particular store, here at Henry's you only have to show up once, or even send another in your place. Then, make your request or bring in your chair or desk for repairs and afterwards I personally deliver it back to the customer." He smiled, placing his hands on the counter as he watched Louis finally make his way to the front of the store.

"You personally deliver to customer's homes?" He asked, amazement in his tone but the truth was in his eyes, he wasn't impressed. Many businesses have started doing this same sort of thing. "How much does one of these custom chairs sell for?" He asked, motioning to the one in the center of the room.

As Henry began to rattle on about prices and the differences in craftsmanship, Louis would make a scan of everything about this man. He wasn't what the barkeep described, he was finely dressed like those of high society in the heart of the city, and was clearly well spoken and educated, but disguises are easy enough, his appearance meant nothing. Again his eyes drifted to the man's fingers, still no blood, as small as the wounds might have been even a little bit would soak through, that was odd, but perhaps he bandages to protect his fingers rather than cover wounds. Henry would step around the counter and escort Louis through the front of the shop going over the unique qualities of each product he had here, and the promise that he could have more made and shipped if need be. It was standing near the smaller man that sparked it, a familiar scent.

Sickly sweet, but leaves a gentle burn in the back of one's throat. That distinct effect of chemicals, but he couldn't place the scent right away, but the memory was there. He'd smelled this not long ago, and suddenly he came to him. The morgue had the same scent, that sickeningly specific smell of fluids and disinfectant, cleaning chemicals for the instruments. This scent was strong on the shopkeeper, but Louis knew it wasn't enough to go on, just a smell, but it was enough to spark suspicion. Perhaps Wilhelm was on to something after all, perhaps this man was involved.

"Will you be buying anything sir?" Henry asked, pulling Louis out of his own thoughts.

"Perhaps." He would bow then. "Allow me time to come back with my Madam, I know she would be thrilled to see this little place, and thrilled even more over such fine furniture." He would chuckle then. "Don't tell her I said this, but her eye for interior design is something to behold."

Henry laughed at Louis' words. "Truly? I thought all women had an eye for such things." He said, clasping his hands in front of him as he watched the other male. "Of course, fetch your Madam and bring her here, I am open for a little while longer today, as well as tomorrow." He then took in a long breath, as though he'd nearly forgotten something. "May I know your Madam's name, just so I know who to keep an eye out for?" He asked, tilting his head slightly.

"Madam J'ai Mauvais." Louis answered quickly, watching as the little man's eyes went from joy to slight shock, and then settled upon what he could only describe as utter delight.

"Oh..." He seemed at a loss for words. "I've heard a little about her, a woman with medical knowledge, a scientific woman. A curious specimen." He said, a soft chuckle escaping him then.

"Yes, my lady has never been one to allow societal norms to hold her back from whatever she wants. I can't tell you how many suitors have tried to whittle their way into Madam Mauvais' heart only to be cast out, but I'm sure I've heard more men tell her she would fail without a husband than men themselves have approached her." Once more he chuckled and would finally open the door. "I shall return with the Madam, if not tonight then first thing in the morning. It's been a pleasure sir." He added with another slight bow.

"The pleasure has been all mine." Henry would wave as the door slowly closed behind Louis. He would watch the other walk out of sight and his smile would quickly fade as his face went stoic. A cold calmness washed over him. "J'ai Mauvais." He whispered the name and turned towards the cabinet in the back. "A gift for my fair lady. Yes, a most perfect gift." He spoke softly, his fingers scratching and pulling at the end of the bandages.

"I don't know why you had to behave that way, the tea was lovely." Wilhelm stated as he walked back into the morgue, carrying a tray with two cups and a kettle resting atop it. "You scared that young cafe worker." He added, placing one of the cups in front of her.

"He was fine." She said, twirling the thread around in her fingers, staring at it, absolutely fixated. "He handled criticism quite well honestly." She added, finally setting the thread down and taking up the kettle and pouring herself a cup.

"He quit." Wilhelm stated.

She coughed while taking a sip of the tea Wilhelm had brought her. "Hm, well, maybe telling him that it was the *worst* tea I've ever had was a bit of a premature statement." She said, gently placing the cup down on the table.

"My tea is lovely! Mother loves my tea…" He muttered the last bit as he sipped from his own cup.

"Mothers are obligated to love everything we do for them." She said with a coy grin as he shot a glare towards her. "As an added statement, your landlord is *not* your mother, despite how she may act or treat you." She stated, crossing her arms as she stared at him.

"Miss Henderson loves it when I call her mother..." Wilhelm muttered somewhat under his breath.

"Miss Henderson has a complex, sexual in nature, and will one day act on this feeling because you keep feeding into her mentality." She brought the tea to her lips once more, though she dreaded taking another sip.

"That's... sick." He visibly shuddered. "Just... be quiet and drink my foul tea." He grumbled as he drank from his own cup.

The day had gone by rather quickly she felt as she looked to the window, the sun setting over the city and the sound of people slowly dying out. She focused on the approaching sound of hooves, listening as they slowed to a stop. She opened her eyes, knowing very well it was Louis, slowly standing at the same time he opened the double doors to the morgue. He was greeted by the surprised gaze of Wilhelm and the expectant eyes of J'ai — he bowed his head softly towards her and approached the table, the body of the man had been moved long ago. To where J'ai didn't know, they probably didn't even know what to do with it given it was a puzzle game of human parts.

"I found something interesting." Louis said, causing her to snap out of her own thoughts.

"What did you find?" The Inspector spoke out before J'ai even had a chance.

"The furniture store lead was good, I found some pubs along the way that knew some of the names of the missing men, and one did mention a strange man watching young Mr. Blithe. As for the store itself, the gentleman there seemed nice enough. Place doesn't get a lot of business, but despite that he informed me that his shop will remain there for as long as he can afford. I assume out of respect and love for someone he lost." He added, turning his eyes to J'ai then, who noted the silent request that lingered in them.

"So you found nothing that the Prim couldn't have found on their own?" She asked suddenly, standing from her seat.

"No, Madam. I did not." He answered, folding his hands behind his back.

"Then we have nothing more to do here." She looked to Wilhelm then. "Inspector, I will continue my own investigation from my manor, inform me of any changes or if another body turns up." She called as she grabbed her coat before heading towards the door. "Let's go home Louis, I need a real cup of tea."

"Yes, Madam." Louis stated, a halfhearted chuckle laced his tone.

There was silence between them as they walked out of the Prim, and into the carriage that waited to take Louis and J'ai back to the manor. She sat with her arms crossed, one leg resting over the other as she stared intently out of the side window. Louis sat in front of her, waiting for the carriage to get moving. He was sure she was thinking about what little they had learned throughout the day, surely she had questions for him. He would be a fool to think she didn't know he had held back some information from Wilhelm upon his return.

"What did you find, Louis?" He was right in his assumption as the question left his mistress.

"I went to a local pub along the docks, as I had told the Inspector. It seemed that the victims had all been patrons at this pub — most if not all of them dock workers or fishermen. He spoke of a man that sat at the back of the pub the night Ichabod went missing but he didn't have more information than that. He did mention a barmaid, a woman by the name of… " He trailed off as he leafed through his notes. "Matilda. No last name was given, but I'm sure we can get one fairly easily." He said, and she hummed thoughtfully.

"Did you talk to her?" She asked, her brow arching curiously.

"No. She was not at the pub. Apparently she took some time off to spend with her lover who only recently returned from-" He was cut off with a swift lift of J'ai's hand.

"I don't care about that, it's not important. We'll go back and find out where she lives and ask her some questions. Barmaids usually see things that sometimes the pub owners do not." She stated, Louis nodding as he flipped through a few pages.

"I then went to the furniture store Wilhelm had pointed out and met a little man by the name of Henry Blithe. A kindly gentleman with a good eye for quality… though I don't see him being the man we're looking for." Louis stated.

"Why?" She asked without tearing her gaze from the window.

"He had plenty of bandages on his fingers—the man we're looking for has a much steadier hand. He wouldn't prick his fingers nearly as often, if at all." He explained—shaking his head.

"Unless he's smart." J'ai stated — finally looking over to Louis with a smirk. "I would put bandages on to divert attention from me. Anything else stand out about this shop, or the little man?" She asked, leaning back into the seat.

"The shop had a familiar chemical smell the closer you got to the counter. The furniture was well stitched — seamlessly from what I could tell. Beyond the bandages, he could be a good one to look into. Though I didn't see much just from looking around." He said, shrugging softly.

"We'll have a look." She said, "First the barmaid though. I want all the information possible." She stated, and soon the carriage came to a slow stop in front of the manor. "Finally, tea and some supper." She chirped, hopping out of the car.

"You seem to be enjoying this, my lady. You're happier than usual." Louis pointed out, following behind her.

"Murder is entertaining, and this just keeps getting more and more interesting." She smiled as they entered the manor. "After supper, back to the East end — and tomorrow, Henry." She finished as he closed the door behind them.

Chapter Six

The sun was beginning to sink below the city; on a normal night this would be the perfect time for J'ai to go digging through a cemetery, but now she was digging through dirt of another sort, carving her way through to the center of this entertaining mystery. She sat in the carriage seat, eyes closed as she thought about the day's events. She was already sure of their culprit, but her own sick sense of entertainment willed her to see this through a little longer, to simply play with the duties given to her. After all, if she were going to be a servant to the Queen herself she was going to do things her way — the fun way.

"This is the address the pub owner gave me." Louis spoke suddenly. Her eyes opened slowly, and she looked out at the shabby little complex cramped between two other, equally shabby looking, buildings.

"Wonderful." She mused to herself as Louis opened the door.

He stepped out first, a light drizzle of rain gently pelted against his head and shoulders before he opened an umbrella. He stood close enough to the carriage that the umbrella would block any rain from hitting J'ai as she stepped out onto the cobblestone walkway. She noted the silent streets with the occasional drunk stumbling along his merry way, and the subtle sounds of people conversing in their homes. However the home they walked upon was not as silent — the bellowing of a male could be heard well out to her carriage, possibly farther.

"Shall I knock?" Louis asked as they approached the door that barely muffled the bellowing man beyond.

"No. I will." She stated as they moved up the four steps in front of the door. She knocked swiftly on the old wood door, and instantly the hollering stopped.

The sound of boots storming towards the door filled her and Louis' ears; unceremoniously the door was flung open and a man with a ragged scar stretching from the left corner of his lip and along the side of his face greeted them. "The 'ell do you want?!" He growled looking down at her.

"I'm here investigating a murder, might I come in and—"

"Get tha fuck off my doorstep!" He interrupted her, then slammed the door harshly in her face.

She was silent, taking in a long breath before, just as slowly, releasing it. "That was very rude." She stated as she turned and took the umbrella from Louis. "Now you may knock, Louis." She added, backing up down the steps slightly as Louis nodded.

"Yes, Madam." Louis stated, giving a slight bow before unbuttoning his jacket and removing it, handing it to J'ai who was already waiting for it to fall into her hand.

"Make sure you subdue him." She added as he turned back to the door.

"Are you sure about this?" Louis asked, loosening his tie slightly.

"The Queen's orders said to solve this by any means necessary." She smirked. "This is by any means, wouldn't you agree?" She asked, and he simply nodded.

He took a stance, and in a single swift motion kicked the door in. The weak hinges gave away easier than he'd expected, causing the door to barely hang from its original position. J'ai had been right about the fisherman not liking the rude entry, but any ideas he had about taking control of the situation were quickly erased as Louis expertly subdued him. The fisherman punched, Louis dipped left and brought the palm of his hand into the bigger man's chin, knocking him back and throwing his guard off long enough for Louis to get another strike to the gut, forcing the other to take a knee. Louis wrapped an arm around the back of the man's throat, holding tightly until the other stopped struggling, finally going limp on the floor as Matilda cried in the background.

"Will!" She called out, daring to try and move to him but stopping when she looked up into the cold gaze of Louis.

J'ai approached her friend and tossed his jacket back at him. She had closed the umbrella when she had come in, and now walked around with it like a cane. Her eyes scanned the woman — she noted the bruises on her arms and along her neck and face. Then her gaze shifted to the man unconscious on the floor — the scar on his face, the booze on his breath and the blood dried on his knuckles. Typical for a man like him, when there is no fish to be caught brawling is the only means to pay for a watered-down mug.

"Who are you people?" She asked, her voice trembling as she watched J'ai move over to the old chair at the center of the room.

She would pat the seat off, and quietly sit herself down holding the umbrella at her front with her hands resting over the handle. "As I tried to tell your... *lover*, I'm investigating a series of murders. The victims all were regulars at the pub you work at." She stated, leaning back into the chair slightly. "The pub owner told us that there was a man who was out of place that went to the bar on the night one of the gentlemen went missing. Do you remember that man?" She asked, her eyes locked on to Matilda at that moment.

There was a pause as she continued to stare at Will, remaining motionless on the floor. "A little bit…" She stated, finally looking at J'ai. "He didn't talk much — the men always talk when they're in a pub. He was a strange fellow though, he didn't even drink. Not much more than water anyway." She sighed softly. "He kept his eyes on the bar, watching Mr. Briggs and Mr. Ichabod. He had left before Ichabod did though, but not long before he did." She said, crossing her arms.

"The pub owner—"

"Mr. Briggs." Matilda cut off Louis suddenly.

"Yes… he said he *thought* he saw him leave after Ichabod." He said, rubbing his chin.

"No, he likely saw my Will leaving. Mr. Briggs drinks a little while working by himself, he barely remembers one night from the next." Matilda stated, shaking her head slowly.

"Can you tell us what the man looked like? Assuming you were close enough, and sober enough, to get a good eye on him." J'ai asked, waving the unimportant information away.

"Messy hair, and a scruffy beard. He wore a suit, a bit wrinkled but it was tailored well enough I suppose." She hummed thoughtfully for a moment. "Oh, and he had bandages on his fingers. I remember because he kept grabbing me when he wanted something rather than calling out like the others normally do." She said, her shaking head slowly.

"Likely didn't want to draw attention to himself by calling out." J'ai said, rubbing her chin slowly.

"Henry doesn't have a beard, Madam." Louis stated, looking

over to her — all he was greeted with was a coy smirk.

"Thank you, miss." J'ai would say suddenly, standing from her seat then. "You've given us more information than the pub—" She caught herself. "Mr. Briggs has given." She finished, and then motioned towards Louis. "I'll send someone to repair the door." She looked at the man on the floor and shook her head. "Miss, you are a well spoken young lady. Too good for a man like him, do yourself a favor…" She trailed off as she opened the umbrella on the doorstep as she stepped out into the rain once more. "Gather what money you have lying about, and whatever he may have dusting the walls of his pockets, and get out of this town." She would turn her back on the woman then, and head back towards the carriage.

"Parting words of wisdom is unlike you." Louis pointed out as he took the umbrella from J'ai then as she opened the carriage door.

"Words of wisdom are seldom heeded." She replied. "I wasted effort is more accurate." She added, crossing her arms over her chest as he climbed in the carriage behind her.

"Is it so hard to admit that even you care sometimes?" Louis asked with a smirk as he closed the door

She didn't respond — she just motioned for him to give the driver the order to head back home. The day had ended, and she was ready to call it a day. Whatever happened tonight was none of her concern until morning came. She expected something to happen — the true surprise would be if nothing happened at all. She doubted that though. Her eyes turned out the small window at the side of the carriage, the rain sticking to the heavy glass and obscuring any imagery beyond its lens. Despite anything she might say to the contrary, her mind lingered on the bruises of the barmaid, Matilda. Her final words to a woman she'd likely never see again, yet a familiar feeling enveloped her. A sense of obligation, even if it was only in the form of venom-laced advice. Advice that would likely go unheeded; her part in it was finished though, tomorrow she would finally meet Henry.

The pub stood oddly silent tonight against a misty backdrop. Light flickered in the windows of the pub as Mr. Briggs did his nightly routine around the bar. He poured himself a tall glass of gin and downed half of it in one go. It was a slow night, and only seemed to be getting slower ever since the disappearances and now murders. He sighed softly and leaned against the counter, a rough hand rubbed worriedly against his forehead. He stared at his reflection in the liquid in his cup, his hands trembling as he sat in the sickening silence, until he heard the sound of the door opening and hitting against the sidewall next to the door.

His eyes fell upon a small, well dressed man that stood in front of the door as it slowly closed behind him. Mr. Briggs' brows furrowed as he brought the cup to his lips and downed the rest of it before quietly filling it up again. The man stepped into the light, revealing himself to be Henry Blithe, and calmly sat down at the bar right in front of the other man. He produced another cup and sat it in front of Henry, who watched as the cup was also filled to the brim with gin. He nodded his head and took the cup, bringing it to his lips and taking a small sip before setting it back down in front of him.

"Evenin' Henry." Briggs stated, another half mug of gin down.

"Hello, Eddy." Henry replied as he just watched the other.

"I've had some time to think on yer words, Henry." He said, nodding his head softly. "Yer right, we did wrong by you and that other fairy." He said, shaking his head slowly.

"His name was Samuel." Henry stated, glaring at the other then as he gripped the cup. "On top of that, you did way worse. More than a pitiful apology from a drunk that doesn't even believe his own words." He stated.

"Henry—" He was cut off as the mug hit him in the side of the head, causing him to fall to the floor.

"You *watched*." Henry hissed as he walked around the bar.

"Wait a minute—" He whimpered when the other man stood over him, a seam-ripper pressed to his neck with a trembling hand.

"You watched while they destroyed something so *beautiful*." Henry spoke through grit teeth.

"Henry — please, I didn't do nothin'." Eddy began to blubber. "I didn't touch 'im!" He added, looking right into the other's eyes.

"That's right. You did nothing." Swiftly he pulled his free hand from his jacket pocket and pressed a rag over Eddy's mouth. "You just watched, then you lied to the constables about what happened, and continued to spout your ugly, hateful words!" Eddy had gone limp under him as he'd finished. "Now... Now I will make you beautiful, Eddy." He whispered, taking hold of the larger man's pant legs and dragging him out of the back of the building.

Chapter Seven

J'ai sat silently in the dining room, a thoughtful silence would hang over her as she sipped from her cup, and picked at the breakfast provided to her. Caroline stood in the background, quietly hidden behind the door as she watched her Madam sit in this choking silence. She took a breath and stepped into the room, a tray and a fresh kettle of tea placed upon it. She was an odd one, this much she'd known for herself since she was a young girl. Ever since she was little she'd always seen things — colors, but not like an aura like some people claim to see; no, it was different. It only happened at certain times and under certain circumstances. The colors came from voices, tones and the like.

"Thank you, Caroline." J'ai would speak, a dark, almost blood red color seemed to outline the words that left her lips.

"You're welcome." She would bow her head softly, and then just watch the other woman for a moment. "You seem… in an oddly good mood." She would state, merely pointing out her own observations.

"Today promises to be an interesting one." J'ai replied as she motioned for Caroline to refresh her cup.

Red had many meanings, but that wasn't the point of her personal feelings towards it. Since she'd come here J'ai had never had a color that laced her words. They had always been gray and empty, like her, a mystery to Caroline from the day she met her and yet suddenly color filled the Madam's life. Did such horrible things truly bring life to her? It seemed cold, then again this was J'ai, and Louis had warned her before he'd even brought her here that the lady of the house was a bit distant.

"Are you going to stand there all morning while I have my breakfast?" J'ai's words brought her back to reality causing her to jump a little.

"I'm sorry!" She chirped then. "I'll go back to my other duties!" She began to hurry away then, but was stopped when she felt J'ai's hand grip her arm.

"Caroline..." J'ai trailed off as she said her name. "Were you around when that man dropped off that letter for me by chance?" She asked, staring back into Caroline's eyes when the girl looked at her.

"No... I was cleaning in another room, I hadn't even heard anyone knock if I'm honest ma'am." She answered, and J'ai released her.

"Keep an eye out for him in the future, a man in a white suit. I'd like your opinion of him." She would state, and then wave her hand for the girl to leave then as she went back to her breakfast.

She would nod and take the now empty tray back towards the kitchen with her. Caroline furrowed her brows thoughtfully as she placed the tray down on the counter. She came to this place knowing nothing about her Madam — with most people it was simple to read them, the colors told her all she needed to know about anyone as long as they were speaking. She knew when they were lying, or when they were honest. She even knew when they were scared. She never saw anything like that with J'ai, so it was hard to tell when the woman was being honest or dishonest with her — it was hard to tell anything about her at all. She had to learn for herself how confident and stubborn J'ai really was, how cold she could be, and yet kind at the same time. She was a passionate person when it came to certain things — this she had learned getting to know the woman, but there was still so much she didn't know, didn't understand.

Like why she had done what she did in the past, it was almost enough to make Caroline pack up and leave. Something so disturbing, so monstrous… she couldn't possibly stay here. Yet, she did, because something inside her told her that there was more to the story. It didn't make it any more right or wrong, but there had to be a good reason and she truly wanted to find out. Asking, however, was out of the question. She'd thought about asking Louis — J'ai's time locked away, she had gotten closer to Louis who was far more open about his feelings and personal self than J'ai was. At the end of the four months they'd gotten far closer than she'd have guessed they would have yet they both knew they had to remain professional while performing their duties. It was because of this that the thought of picking his mind about their Madam crossed her mind, but she didn't wish to test his loyalty to the woman, that would be rude of her.

A frantic knock came at the door, and she moved from the kitchen, wiping her hands on her apron as she approached the entrance hall. Louis had already approached the door, slowly pulling it open as a young woman pushed in past him. He blinked, and closed the door before following her; he looked at her like he knew her, and this confused Caroline for a moment as he reached out and gently took hold of her wrist, stopping the woman from proceeding any further into the mansion. She struggled, and spoke frantic nonsense as she desperately tried to pull away from his grasp.

"That is quite enough, Matilda." Louis snapped, jostling her wrist to force her to focus. "You can't just barge—"

"Mr. Briggs is gone!" She cried out, falling to her knees as Louis continued to hold on to her.

"Gone?" Louis questioned, and then sighed as he knelt down to the floor on one knee. He was far more gentle now as he switched the position of his hand on her wrist, to her shoulder. "Did you run all the way here?" He asked then, switching the topic for now. As she was she couldn't be much in the way of help. She was far too frantic now, and Caroline could see it, frantic and afraid — no, worried.

"Come on then." Caroline spoke suddenly, holding her hand out for the woman to take. "Let's get you to the kitchen and get you something to sip at while you calm yourself. Louis will inform the Madam of your arrival." She said, offering the young woman a kind smile.

It took Matilda a few moments before she shakily took the other woman's hand and nodded. Louis merely observed, watching Caroline carefully as she slowly moved the other woman into the kitchen area, her eyes glancing back for only a moment to silently tell him she would take care of the strange girl. Louis would turn towards the dining room then, fix his sleeves, and then step into the room and approach J'ai — her eyes were already directed towards him, seemingly knowing something had happened at that moment.

"Matilda is here. She said the pub owner was missing." He stated, getting right to the point.

"Any bodies turn up?" She asked, pushing her plate away from her.

"It doesn't seem so." He replied swiftly. "It is still early though." He added as she stood from her chair.

"I think our Dollmaker would rather do his work at night." She said, and then shrugged. "Oh well, no body to be found but a man has gone missing. It seems he is still busy." She crossed her arms as she stood before Louis. "Where is

69

Matilda?" She asked.

"The kitchen." He answered simply.

She marched towards the kitchen, Louis grabbing her dirty plate and cup and following behind her. Matilda had calmed somewhat since she'd been left with Caroline — an interesting gift it seemed, but it would all come crashing down in a moment's breath it seemed. She saw J'ai enter the room and she practically lunged at the other woman, gripping her shoulders as she began to shake. She repeated the blubber about Mr. Briggs and pressed her face into J'ai's shoulder as she began to sob once more. She turned and looked back to Louis who simply stared back awkwardly, unsure himself of what to do in this situation.

"Miss… please, stop." J'ai stated coldly, pushing the woman back slightly. "Stop sobbing. How are you certain that your boss went missing?" She asked, rubbing the bridge of her nose.

"I went to the pub this morning. Doing what you'd said, I gathered up all I could and I plan to move into the city." She sighed softly. "I was going to go tell him goodbye, but instead I found the bar in shambles, and a note." She explained, gripping her arms in an attempt to keep herself grounded.

"Did you bring the note?" J'ai asked, crossing her arms.

"No. I ran straight here, but I can tell you what it said." She stated, watching as J'ai nodded for her to repeat the note. "It said: 'I will make the world as beautiful as he was.'" She said, looking between the three before her for even a hint if they knew what that meant.

"Interesting." Was all J'ai said.

70

"My good friend is in danger and that is all you have to say?! He's likely dead and I'm wasting time on someone like you!" She growled, forcing J'ai to arch a brow.

"I'm sure he's alive." She added, shaking her head as the woman continued to cry, though only a little now.

"How can you be sure?" Matilda asked, trembling slightly as she turned her eyes to the floor. "Those other men turned up dead." She added, swallowing back tears.

"Not all of them. There is still what remains of Ichabod." She reminded the girl, though she'd forgotten that was something she hadn't been aware of.

"What remains of him?" She questioned, a look of shock in her eyes then.

"Miss, how about something to drink. Calm your nerves." Caroline interrupted then. "The Madam will take care of it, I'm sure." She added, quickly leading the woman away from the room then.

"You expected a body, but instead you have a kidnapping, it seems." Louis stated as he rinsed the plate and the cup quickly.

"Full of surprises, isn't he?" She chuckled. "Let's go to the pub, see if we can't find anything else before heading to the furniture repair." She stated, already heading for the staff exit.

"Not going through the dining room?" Louis asked, following behind her as he dried his hands.

"Risk facing that mess again? No thank you." She replied as the two stepped out once more.

"Help! Anyone, please, help me!"

Eddy's voice cried out from within the cramped metal drawer — it was cold, and no matter where he moved the bare skin of his body got no relief. He thrashed violently, and screamed until he tasted blood in his throat. He didn't know how long he'd been in here, at some point he just stopped caring and stopped screaming. He closed his eyes, thinking back on the night that seemingly laid out the path that put him in this position. The faces of the regular folk that wandered into his pub in the late hours of the evening. How was he to know what would have happened that night? How would he have known it would land him here?

He had been drinking with them, laughing about some foolish thing, he couldn't remember, not that it was important but it was a distraction to draw out the memory. He wanted to go back, and stop Ichabod from what he was about to do. The man walked into the pub to escape the rain that night, he was nice enough, but everyone knew what he was. He did tell them to leave the man alone, he told them — he tried, he truly did. It wasn't enough. He remembered watching them drag him out back, screaming as his jacket tore on a nail at the corner of the back door. The rest was a blur, a flurry of fists and blood, and he just stood there as this poor boy was beaten to death outside his pub.

"*You bloody idiots!*" He had yelled at them. "*Lookit what ya done! Don't just stand there, get on wit it and get 'im outta my alleyway!*" He sighed, and opened his eyes slowly.

"… I right fucked up this time, didn't I?" He spoke to himself, and then kicked the hatch below his feet. "Oi! Let me outta here! Face me like a man ya goddamn fairy!" He bellowed, knowing his wording wouldn't go over well, but surprisingly there was no movement outside, only silence.

There was a clattering next to him, he jumped and pressed himself against the opposite wall of the drawer as he saw a small medallion slip through a small hole in the corner of his compact and cold cell. Recognizing it, he relaxed then tried to shift in a way to maybe look through the hole before the medallion was awkwardly pulled back through; he was greeted by a bloodshot green eye, and again he jumped a little but peered right back.

"… Ichabod? Lad, is that you?" There was a struggling and muffled voice from the other side, like something preventing him from speaking. "Knock if it's you, boy." A knock immediately followed. "Are you okay?" The silence he took for a no. "… Did… did he cut ya?" There was a knock, and his heart fell. "… I'm glad ya alive at least." He said, his jaw clenched as he fought back the panic.

It was then, like a sick joke, that the sound of someone approaching could be heard. The medallion slid into his space once more, and he stared at it for a moment before looking to the hole with the eye that peered back at him. He saw tears — a desperate and pleading look, and instantly he knew. Henry didn't come for him when he hollered because he had to finish with another first. Quickly he tried to push the medallion back, as if that in some way would prevent Henry from taking him, but he saw the little stream of light beam through the hole, and the panicked muffled scream of Ichabod as he was pulled from his drawer.

"No… NO!" Eddy screamed as he thrashed about in his own drawer. "Ya leave 'im alone ya fuckin' bastard!" White hot tears began to stream down his face as he heard the faint sound of his friend struggling.

Metal tools clinked, pained moans following before silence. A silence more deafening than anything he'd heard before.

This was their fault. This was happening because of their own choices. It wasn't fair — it wasn't fair. He clenched his eyes shut as the thought repeated itself in his own head, pleading to a God he wasn't sure was even listening anymore, and like a child he found that his final thoughts were that of home and the desire to be there; anywhere else other than here. This place where the smell of blood hangs in the air, a place he was sure he would die and no one would ever know.

"Please! Someone help us!!"

Chapter Eight

Hunger. Thirst.

These were the two main things that ached him now, alongside the wondering of how long he'd been inside the metal box. Packed within like a forgotten shame he would simply lie there, staring blankly upward as dried streaks from tears stained his face. In the silence that followed Ichabod's departure, a part of him knew the man was dead now. He was left to wonder when it would be his turn to be dragged from this compact cell, to be tortured or whatever it was that he did to poor Ichabod. He closed his eyes,fighting back more tears, knowing very well his fate was likely going to be the same as the younger man, and suddenly all his life's regret washed over him. The wives he laid around on, the children he abandoned over his years… He was truly a horrible excuse of a man.

"Forgive me Father, for I 'av sinned — I've not been an honest or true man in me years on your Earth. I've abandoned all forms of responsibility, and hid away in a rottin' hole in the ground and didn't care 'bout who I might'a been hurtin'. Forgive me my transgressions and walk with me in this hour of need, 'an I swear, Lord God, if I live to see another day this man will change. In the name of the Father, the son and the Holy spirit, amen." He crossed over his chest and sighed softly.

There was time, how much time he couldn't be certain, but enough time to pass after the prayer for him to collect himself once more. He heard the distant sound of keys jingling, then a door opening. The sound of shoes against hard stone flooring as they grew closer and closer with each passing moment; his chest tightened as they stopped in front of his coffin-like cell. He heard the keys again, and one entered the lock of his drawer before violently swinging open, allowing the light from outside to pool in and force him to shy his gaze away from the pain of not being in the light for Lord knows how long.

"Henry!" Eddy exclaimed as he was dragged from the drawer. "Enough of this! All this ain't gonna bring him back!" He yelled, struggling slightly as the smaller male pulled him fully out of the drawer.

"I know." Was all Henry would reply with as he jerked the larger male onto the gurney in front of him. "The doll will be quiet and still now." He ordered, holding a sharp blade to Eddy's throat as he pushed him over to the center of the room.

"Then… why? Just for revenge?" He asked, never taking his eye off the blade.

"Dolls don't speak — they are silent, and still." The knife pressed into his throat slightly. "Silent… and still." He repeated harshly.

Eddy gasped at the feel of the blade slowly digging into his neck, then he sighed and resigned to whatever may come. He'd made his peace with God, with himself, and though he looked back on everything and regretted all of it there was no turning back the clock or even apologizing for that matter. He would grunt as he was pushed onto another table, another sound of surprise leaving him when Henry grabbed his face and forced him to look up at the other male, and he saw that clear look of confusion. He expected the fight, to have to tell him over and over to be quiet like he had to do with the others, and had he been any younger maybe he would be bellowing like a child, but he'd been alive too long to be afraid of dying at this point.

He thought of Matilda in that moment, tears welling in his eyes as he stared upward. He felt Henry jerking his arm around but he didn't react to the touch, he wasn't afraid anymore. What was the point? He closed his eyes, and thought about all the things he'd wished to say to the girl that worked for him, how proud he was of her. She had come a long way from that dirty little girl that he caught stealing from his kitchen, he hoped she knew she could do whatever she put her mind to, and knew she could do better than that pitiful man of hers. In a perfect world… he could tell her that.

A searing pain interrupted his thoughts, metal grinding against his flesh caused him to jerk and flail on the table, but Henry was oblivious it seemed to the other's agony. In his hand he worked a saw through flesh — tendons, muscle and bone, and Eddy couldn't help but focus on the disgustingly wet and grinding sound the teeth of the saw-blade made as it chewed violently through his limb. He cried out, finally screaming once more for help, begging for mercy as the pain shot through him like lightning. Henry smiled a toothy smile, like that of a mischievous child who just shaved the house cat; yes, this was what he had wanted.

The screams of terror, the pleading. It was all the same orchestra he was sure Samuel had sang out for the ones that hurt him. Begging for them to stop, pleading with them, and that drove him — the fire inside him spread further and further with each push of the saw through flesh. His own tears began to pour down his cheeks at the thought of the suffering his love had to face, his usual steady hand became shaky, his movements more violent. He began to grunt angrily as he passed the blade through the final sections of flesh, ending with the arm falling limp onto a tray beneath him. He panted, the sound of Eddy sobbing barely breaking through to him as he stared at the ragged end of the dismembered arm.

"Sloppy." Is all he said in a soft tone, then his gaze turned to Eddy who stared back with a shaken gaze. "Dolls are silent and still. Dolls don't feel pain, and dolls don't cry." He gripped his hand around Eddy's mouth, holding him there as his fingers dug violently into the other man's face. "Silence and beauty — I will give you this, Eddy." He whispered with a crazed gaze.

A soft ringing would echo through the room at that moment, the sound of a bell from the floor above signaled a guest on the top floor. His eyes narrowed in aggravation from the disturbance this presented, but quickly came out of it when he remembered who the guest might be. He smiled and quickly released Eddy's face with a slight push that made his head bounce off the table. Quickly he wrapped the wound, the bandage staining red almost immediately, and then he placed a ball of fabric into Eddy's mouth to keep him silent while he was away, finally strapping him down to the table.

"Be a doll — be silent." He said before quickly making his way to the door. He stopped briefly to remove the bloodstained apron and adjust the sleeves to his suit, before stepping back into the main room of his store. "I'm sorry, I hope you haven't been waiting long." Eddy would hear him say as he went into the shop above.

He watched as that door slowly closed him down into this tomb, his face pale and his eyes shaking as he fought the urge to pass out. He heard the muffled voices from above, a familiar tone filtered through to him but his mind was too hazy to place it. He turned his head slightly, quickly jumping, or trying to, when he came practically face to face with the lifeless eyes of Ichabod. He couldn't control it, the muffled screams filtered from within him — he almost didn't believe the sounds were coming from him. He struggled,causing the table to jostle slightly, and creak under the weight of his violent movements. The table would snap after a moment and crash loudly on the floor,the rag placed in his mouth went loose and he managed to spit it out.

"Help me!" His voice was dry and hoarse but he pushed through. "Please! I'm here!! Help me!"

The sky had darkened over the city, and it had begun to rain softly. The sound of droplets pattering against the roof of the carriage echoed in both passengers' ears. J'ai thought about the girl, Matilda, and her desperate need to find her boss. It struck her a little odd that anyone from the East End would care as much for their slum-boss the way she cared for Mr. Briggs. Not that it mattered, but J'ai, surprisingly, was human, and oftentimes curiosity about the lives others led filled her mind. Many would say she was cold for letting something so unimportant fill her thoughts — especially in the midst of all that was happening now.

"Madam?" Her eyes turned to Louis then, who stared back with an almost concerned gaze. "You've been oddly silent since we started towards the shop." He said, his arms remained crossed over his chest as he eyed her.

"Something is odd. It might not be important, but it bothers me." She said as she rubbed her chin thoughtfully.

"What is odd?" He asked with a casual tone.

"Matilda. Her concern for her boss is strange." She answered his question, her tone as casual as his own, as though they were merely conversing about the weather.

"Is it? She seems like the kind of woman that would worry about those around her. Even you maybe." He chuckled when her eyes snapped to him then. "Is it so out of the question that a person could care for another without an ulterior motive?" He asked, shrugging slightly.

"I suppose not… but it all seems strange to me. It doesn't add up somehow." She leaned back with a huff and crossed her arms. The rain that had pattered lightly before now beat against the roof with more force as the downpour increased. "Louis… tell the driver to hurry along faster to that pub — Mr. Brigg's pub." She stated, pointing to the little sliding window behind Louis.

"Of course, Madam, but… why the rush all of a sudden?" Louis asked, turning to do as he was told.

"I'll explain later, just trust me." She didn't have to tell him to trust her — of course he already did.

Their stop came up quickly; the pub sat in a strange silence. Louis moved for the umbrella, his head snapping towards J'ai as she opened the carriage door and hopped out, moving towards the pub in the pouring rain. He followed after her, leaving the umbrella behind in that moment as they went inside the building. J'ai looked around slowly as she approached the bar — two glasses remained on the bar, one had been toppled. She assumed it had been Mr. Brigg's glass given it was on the bartender's side — obviously Briggs had been surprised — based on the bar-stool knocked back to the floor. The interaction happened quickly.

She stepped around the bar and knelt down where the spilled alcohol would have likely dripped off the edge of the counter. There was nothing though, there would have been stains left behind given how long the alcohol would have rested. She hummed softly and stood back up and looked around slowly, her eyes coming to a stop on another cup sitting near a wash-tub alongside other dishes. She approached the cup and picked it up, giving the rim of the glass a sniff, furrowing her brows in that moment. She stared at the cup and grazed her thumb over the rim of the cup, it was faint and smudged but there was a hint of rouge on the glass and slowly a new piece to the puzzle was presented to her.

"Louis do you remember if Matilda mentioned having a drink before she ran to the manor?" J'ai asked, keeping her gaze on the cup.

"I don't believe she mentioned it." Louis replied with a quick shrug. "Why do you ask?" Louis moved closer as J'ai placed the cup back down.

"That cup has the remains of rouge on it, which means a woman obviously drank from that cup and quickly cleaned it. Not very well, but they cleaned it none-the-less." She stated, and then motioned to the other cups on the counter. "However that cup wasn't used until after whatever happened at the bar was already over, on top of that the mess from the toppled glass had been cleaned. Not a stain anywhere, counter or floor." She would then motion around them, Louis' eyes following her motions. "There is also something missing from here, something Matilda told us would be here." She said and for a moment, Louis was confused.

"The note." He realized suddenly, looking back to J'ai then who nodded.

"Exactly." She said while crossing her arms.

"Perhaps she grabbed it after-all and forgot about it." He said, furrowing his brows.

"I doubt it, given she remembered well enough what it said word for word." J'ai added.

"She was so distraught though, shaking like a leaf." He said, and then motioned with his hand towards J'ai then.

"What about Caroline? She wouldn't be able to lie around her, you and I both know that." He said and shook his head. "She can't be involved."

"The distraught behavior was honest, not because she was worried for Mr. Briggs though." She smiled then as Louis readied himself. "She's in on this, all of it. She is connected to the Doll-maker — how I don't know yet but she *is* connected. She lied about the note, and was more than likely here while Mr. Briggs was being taken out the back. It's possible she even helped move the man, which would explain why she would need a quick drink from the bar. Nerves would also explain the lack of a stain on the floor or counter from the spilling drinks — she cleaned it up." Louis sighed and rubbed the back of his neck. "Think about it. Matilda likely knew all of the missing men, if not directly then because of her connection with the pub — she'd know their comings and goings better than anyone. The large tips from the stranger and the mismatched stories from her and Mr. Briggs about the night Ichabod went missing." She moved past Louis then. "She was able to fool Caroline because her emotions were honest, she was afraid. Not afraid of losing Mr. Briggs though, afraid of being caught."

"So… she is working with the Dollmaker?" He slowly followed her and got lost in his own thoughts as he tried to piece it together for himself.

"Something connects them, that much I know." She said, climbing back into the carriage. "What connects them we won't find out until the end." Her smile was growing, she seemed excited now as they prepared to continue towards the shop.

"Entertaining?" Louis asked as he sat in the seat across from her.

"Very much so." She replied as the carriage creaked back

to life as it began moving once more towards their final stop.

Henry's Comfort Design and Repair.

Chapter Nine

The weather seemingly got worse the moment they came to a stop in front of the store. This time Louis was ready with the umbrella as the two stepped out of the carriage, the rain bouncing heavily off of the canopy as they walked up to the door of the store. She stepped inside, Louis closing the umbrella and following in behind her. She scanned around the room briefly, then moved to eye some of the furniture as it seemed Henry wasn't around, or so it would appear. The two would only eye one of the chairs briefly before they heard a soft click and they turned around to see Henry moving from behind the counter.

"I'm sorry about that. I was downstairs, working on a project for a client." He explained, holding his hand out towards J'ai. "Your servant was here yesterday — he told me I should expect him to return with you." He said, offering her a kindly smile.

"Yes, Louis told me about your little shop here. I wasn't expecting such a nice store in such a poor neighborhood." She chided, motioning around slightly. "Though from the outside you wouldn't even know this place was here — blends in very well." She saw him clench his jaw slightly. "Must deter thieves and all sorts of criminals from the outside alone." She added with a coy smirk.

A low thoughtful hum was all Henry replied with in that moment, but she could see the pounding of anger behind the look in his eyes. Louis kept a close eye on him — though he knew there was nothing he could really do to harm J'ai it was still his job to prevent anything from happening to her, and added to his job was keeping her from making the same mistakes she had in the past. His gaze would leave her then, and turn towards Henry — his eyes fell down to the man's hands and took note of the lack of bandages. His fingers were pristine, not so much as pin-prick let alone scars from countless mistakes made.

He was about to question this when the crash came from the room below — followed by the cries for help, and he made a move towards the counter but froze when he heard the sharp tone of Henry. "Don't!" He exclaimed. "I swear, I'll slit her damn throat!" He hissed as he held the seam cutter to J'ai's throat at that moment. "Don't move a muscle." He repeated the warning, pressing it deeper into her skin.

Louis stared at him, then to J'ai who stared back with a stoic gaze. "Unfortunately, sir, by the Queen's orders we must see this through." His eyes went back to J'ai then. "By *any* means necessary." With that he continued forward.

"No!" Henry yelled, then looked to J'ai. His eyes passed back and forth between them, his heart racing. "I'll kill her! Leave it be damn it!"

"You can't stop him." J'ai would say suddenly. "Only I can." She smirked.

"Tell him to be still! I will kill you I—"

"Swear to God?" She asked, looking at him from the corner of her eye. "If God were real do you truly believe he would have allowed this to go on as long as it did, or to even begin at all? God has no say in what happens, not in this world or the next." She felt the knife pressing into her, his hand shaking.

Henry's mind snapped to attention when he heard the familiar click of the door behind the counter, his face going pale as he watched Louis descend the steps. He heard Mr. Briggs below, crying tears of joy at the prospect of being saved. It was all for nothing. That was the first thing that went through Henry's mind, followed quickly by the face of the man that he had been doing this all for. His heart almost stopped, he felt like it could have — then all fear left him and then his hand glided across J'ais neck with the blade. Flaying it open, wide for the world to see. It was like slow motion as she slumped to the floor, choking as blood pooled from her neck.

"No one will stop me from making him truly beautiful. No one." He moved towards the door, closing it behind him and locking it before he continued forward.

Reaching the bottom of the stairs, he looked around before down to the floor. Blood stained the ground there,wet and fresh and trailed off to the far back corner of the room behind the wall where he finished his dolls. A curtain blocked the view of the other side, and as he got closer he grunted out as he ripped it down and saw only a half conscious Briggs on the floor, the side of his body drenched with blood. If he didn't get the wound closed soon the man would bleed to death — he would be useless then, he had to be alive to suffer properly. It was a brief moment of thought before he remembered Louis, and quickly turned around in time for the man to knock the blade from his hand and punch him.

 He would grunt and stumble back, knocking over vials of chloroform and cleaning fluids from his work table. He brought his hand to his face and drew it back to see the blood and growled, grabbing one of the vials and throwing it at Louis forcing him to block as the vial of liquid hit him, some of the contents spilling on his sleeve before shattering on the floor at his feet. He lowered his arms and Henry was at him — jabbing at him with a scalpel now, forcing him to back away. Henry made a wild swipe, catching the other man's arm and easily slicing through his sleeve and to his skin. Louis hissed and then pushed forward with a heavy kick, knocking Henry down and to the floor this time.

"Enough of this." Louis growled, moving to stand over him.

"I agree." Henry replied, crawling forward and grabbing the seam ripper.

Louis grabbed him, putting him in a chokehold and fastening his grip firmly around the other's throat. The two struggled as Henry fought desperately for air, flailing his blade around wildly in that moment. His vision was blurring, and his limbs were getting weaker — he couldn't go out like this, not like this. He hit something then, and suddenly Louis' arms went slack around him and he gasped for air as he pulled himself forward, loosening his tie as he caught his breath. Henry sighed, and flopped back onto the ground to collect himself then — but with a quick regain of energy he growled and sat up, shifting over to Louis and sitting on his chest as he began to stab him over and over again.

"Should have listened!" He exclaimed with each stab before finally relaxing. "I have to be quick now." He spoke, thinking out loud as his eyes darted towards Sam's drawer. "We have to leave." He whispered and stood up, hurrying over to the metal drawer and quickly opening it. He pulled the slab out of the drawer and took in a sharp breath when he saw the slab was empty — Sam's body was gone. "No...!" He said, placing his hands on the cold table as though to make sure he wasn't seeing things.

"Sorry Henry." He turned towards the familiar feminine voice — his eyes widening as he saw J'ai standing there at the bottom of the stairs. Sam's corpse sat neatly on the bottom step and leaned against the wall as though he were merely asleep at that moment. "I'm surprised you believed it would be that easy."

The blade in his hand clattered to the floor, and he slumped to his knees. "Please... don't hurt him." He begged, his eyes only on Sam.

"You can't hurt a corpse, Henry." She said as she turned to look down at the young man wrapped in the white sheet. "I think I understand now, seeing him for myself." Her eyes went back to Henry, defeated and sobbing on the floor. "I can understand killing the men that hurt him, but why Mr. Briggs?" She asked, looking towards the dying man on the other side of the room. "Right — I almost forgot about him. Henry, will you take care of the man's arm?" She asked, moving forward and lifting him from the ground. "Come on, enough sobbing. It's over now." She added, and he took in a sharp breath.

"I suppose it is…" He said, then turned his eyes to her throat. "How? There isn't even a mark and I watched your throat practically split open." He finally questioned it. "I had heard rumors… but I hardly believed it." He continued.

"It isn't important how — the only thing that matters is that it happened. Rumors, however, can be muddied. I'm sure half of what you heard wasn't even true." She stated, guiding him towards Eddy then.

"You survived a burning." He said, even his tone remained defeated.

"Alright, well, that bit is true." She looked to Louis then, and swiftly kicked his foot. "Get up — you've laid around enough." She stated and turned back to Henry and Eddy.

"I suppose, but it's rare I get a chance to relax like this." He stated, sitting up.

"What are you people?" Henry asked as he cleaned Eddy's wound.

"Cursed." Is all J'ai said in reply. "Now, answer my questions and get that man fixed up." She ordered, waving her hand as a sign for him to hurry.

There was a long silence from Henry as he turned his eyes towards Eddy unconscious before him, and his blood began to boil even before he began speaking. "Edward Briggs..." His eyes turned back towards Sam. "Samuel Briggs." He said his partner's full name, and both J'ai and Louis perked up at this unexpected news. "Eddy is Sam's father. He hated that Sam was... with me. He believed I corrupted him, and threw him out when Sam refused to leave me and get help for this illness we have." He sighed as he bandaged the man's arm, being a little too rough at times. "Eddy removed Sam from everything, completely disowned his own son because he didn't like who he had fallen in love with."

He stood when he was finished and turned towards J'ai and Louis. "He watched his own son get beaten to death behind his pub, his own flesh and blood. He hated his son so much that he willingly allowed those bastards to murder him!" He exclaimed, fighting back tears.

"No..." They all looked down to Eddy. "I... didn't hate my son. I was afraid for 'im. Afraid of what his choices would mean for 'im..." Mr. Briggs grunted and sat forward, his hand reaching over to his arm. "I didn't stop what had 'appened... 'coz I didn't think he'd die. I thought if I let this 'appen for the reason that it 'appened that he would see his choice was wrong, and that it would only lead to pain... I regret not steppin' in every single day Henry... that choice to stand there ruined everything." He said, and Henry visibly began to shake.

"Do not apologize to me! Apologize to your son and to your daughter!" He exclaimed, pointing an angered finger at Sam.

"Matilda?" J'ai interrupted then, the two males before her looking up to her in that moment. "I had my suspicions — it was only recently I came to that conclusion." She explained, waving her hand.

"Aye, Tilly's me daughter... I'd hoped her workin' in the pub would get her away from that man of hers. I got the same idea in me head when it came to my boy too... but he refused." He sighed and tilted his head back against the dripping counter. "After Sam... she wouldn't even look at me. She had no other job though — so she stayed, but never spoke to me after other than gettin' her pay. Only one died... but I lost both my children 'cause of what I allowed." He shook his head.

"fascinating." J'ai said, though she didn't seem to really care about the speech of regret. "So Matilda accepted the relationship between you and Samuel?" She asked kee,ing her gaze on Henry.

"Yes. Tilly was so sweet — she was even the one that suggested Sam and I stop hiding it from the world. Love was meant to be shared, or something to that effect." He said, waving his hand idly. "That was before anyone outside of the family knew about our relationship." He added, finally standing from the floor.

Louis approached and gripped his upper arm, ready to cart him to Primburogh that very moment. "What about a will? Did Samuel have a will in case anything happened to him?" She asked, causing even Louis to look at her now.

"Yeah – Tilly said it would be a good idea because of the nature of our relationship. That way if anything happened to him I would be able to keep the shop running." He said, also wondering where J'ai was possibly going with this.

"Tilly has seemingly suggested an awful lot, hasn't she?" J'ai asked, but didn't give him time to answer. "She even put the idea of killing everyone that hurt Sam into your head isn't she?" She asked with a smirk.

"No — Tilly wouldn't..." Eddy fell silent even as the words slipped from his lips.

"No, she had nothing to do with this!" Henry exclaimed, stepping forward slightly but was quickly jerked back by Louis. "She was just as hurt about Sam's death as I was!" He added, tears burning in his eyes.

"I'm sure Matilda had everything to gain from the death of her father." J'ai stated, turning her eyes to Eddy then.

"Aye, with Sam dead she'd inherit the pub and whatever money I had left." He said, his eyes lowering to the ground. "She... wouldn't kill me. She can't hate her dad that much... Can she?" He asked seemingly to himself.

"Not just your death, but Sam's as well." J'ai said, and Henry turned his eyes back to her with a snap of his head. "I'm sure you're curious, but really it was obvious from the start — even before Sam's death." She stepped closer to Henry. "She talked him into opening up about his affairs with you. She talked him into setting up that will, and being the smart girl she obviously is she would have had himput her name on it beneath yours. At the time it wouldn't be suspicious, but it should have." Her smirk only grew. "Sam would die, and I'm sure you've not received even a cent yet have you?" She asked and he shook his head. "Of course not, it takes time for a murder victim's inheritance to pay out. Gives her enough time to convince you to start killing people." She said, and the whole time she spoke his eyes lowered to the ground.

"She came to me... not long after I dug up his body..." He said softly. "I thought she would be mad at me when she found him here... but she just smiled. She said she understood the pain I was feeling — she missed him too."

He began to shake.

"She took advantage of your emotional and mental state, Henry. She didn't care at all. Not about you or Sam, only herself and lining her own pockets." She would sigh then. "She was more than likely banking on you being hanged, and the money would be hers. Sam's and her father's." White hot tears spilled down Henry's cheeks. "She used your love for Sam, and his death to try to get money so she could leave town." He snapped his eyes up and locked with hers.

"Liar! You can't possibly know that." Henry said then, in denial till the end.

"I do know, because she came to my manor the morning after helping you move Eddy from the pub." She watched the shock appear in his gaze.

"How do you know she helped me?" He asked, taking a baffled step backwards.

"She left a lot of evidence behind at the pub, she wasn't nearly as careful as you were. She then came to the manor and recited a note you left behind." She added, crossing her arms over her chest.

"There was no note. I didn't leave one." He said, and she nodded.

"Exactly. She made it all up." He seemed like he could collapse in that moment, but he held himself steady. "She wasted no time. She was at my door before I was even finished with breakfast. She plans to leave town; the man she was with likely ships out today or tomorrow given how quickly she acted, which means she probably has a ship ready to sail out herself with what little money she already has." She theorized as Henry became more and more agitated.

"Bitch…" He muttered under his breath, his hands trembling. "That dirty lying *bitch*!" He took in a sharp breath, and tried to calm himself.

"Louis, get Mr. Briggs to a hospital. Then get to Primburogh, and let the Inspector know to send a crew to this shop. Afterwards, you and he meet me personally at the pub." She said, then turned towards Henry.

"Shouldn't I have the Inspector send people to the Pub first?" Louis asked, moving to help Eddy stand. "They should know about Matilda's involvement as well — wouldn't be fair if Henry took all the blame." He said, watching as she put a hand on Henry's shoulder with a smirk.

"Oh, he won't. People will know of Matilda's involvement." She would motion for Henry to follow her. "I'll explain everything on the way. Come on then." She said, everyone filing out of the room.

Henry looked down to Sam as they passed his body on the stairs, he almost tried to break from J'ai in that moment to scoop him up, but he was sure he would be taken care of once the Prim showed up. He hadn't expected this outcome — this woman was far more unique than he had originally thought. Cold, calm, but oddly kind — though she did her best to mask that kindness with harsh descriptors and an air of someone who could ultimately care less. He should have let Sam's death turn him into someone like her, rather than letting a fox like Tilly into the hen-house and convince him to turn into something much worse. He killed, thinking the whole time it was for Sam — that somehow doing those things would make his death mean something. She was using him — the whole time she had her own plan, her own ideas.

He sat in the carriage for what felt like forever until he felt it jerk to a stop; J'ai leaned over briefly and whispered into Louis' ear and silently he nodded before J'ai turned and motioned for Henry to step out of the carriage. He did as he was told, and to his surprise he stepped out in front of Eddy's pub rather than the building of Primburogh. He would turn to meet J'ai as she too stepped from the carriage, watching then as it rode off with Louis and Mr. Briggs still inside. The confusion on his face must have been clear as she would turn and face him then with crossed arms.

"Louis will take Mr. Briggs to a hospital, then go inform Matilda that I need her to come to this location." She said, his eyes widening as he looked at her. "I'm not a copper, I don't pretend to be. I have my own idea of justice, as I'm sure you do." She would produce the seam ripper from within her own jacket and hold it out to him. "There are many things in this world I hate, liars and thieves among the top of the list. Most of all though are people who use the grief of others to do their dirty work." She would place the blade in Henry's hand. "Whatever happens when she arrives, it will be what she deserves. Of that I'm sure." She added — turning then towards the pub so that they could get out of the rain as they waited.

Two days later

The door to her study opened with a soft click — Louis stepped inside and gave a slight bow. "Mr. Cordel is here to speak to you, Madam." He said with a simple tone.

She waved her hand passively and he turned back out of the room, the space empty for only a moment before the man stepped into the space himself. He allowed the door to shut behind him, his hands cupped behind his back as he stared at the back of J'ai's chair. She didn't even dignify him with facing him in that moment, instead she continued to enjoy the view from her window — a rare day with a clear sky — and sip her tea.

"Henry was hanged this morning, and the body of Mr. Brigg's son was properly put to rest once more." He stated, straightening the cuffs of his sleeves. "Her Majesty wished for me to come along personally to congratulate you on a job well done." He stated, then slowly approached her desk. "However I have questions about that night and what happened to young Ms. Briggs." His tone was cold as he leaned forward onto the mahogany surface.

Only then she would turn around. "I did explain in my report. He got away before we got to the Prim, tricked her into meeting him at the pub. We had no idea he'd doubled back on us like that." She answered simply.

"She said she saw you there." He narrowed his eyes to her, looking for any crack in the other's gaze.

"She must be mistaken. I wasn't there until after it was all over, when I finally realized what was happening." He growled and stood straight, crossing his arms over his chest.

"Eyelids removed, lips carved to the bone. Her nose, and several layers of flesh removed from her face. The woman will never be able to go out in public again because of what he did to her and right to the end he never said why. Why her, J'ai?" She looked up to him when he posed this question to her.

She shrugged, leaning back in her chair. "I haven't the faintest, Simon." She answered, but of course he didn't believe a word of it. "Does it matter in the end? So a girl's face was ruined and a man lost an arm. Be glad they are alive at all, and the man responsible is on the ground. It's all the Queen really cares about after all, isn't it?" She asked, and he huffed out of annoyance.

"We'll be in touch — the Queen always has jobs on hand. If I were you though, I'd not let what happened to Ms. Briggs become a recurring theme in your investigations in the future… Lady Mauvais." He finished, bidding her farewell with a quick bow before pushing past Louis in the hallway and away from this place.

Louis stepped inside, closing the door quietly behind him. He stepped up to the desk and stood next to J'ai as he watched Mr. Cordel climb into his carriage and ride away, likely back to the palace. His attention then turned down to J'ai, who calmly sipped her tea and smirked to herself. Clearly she was proud of that little display of hers, and proud to know that Mildred would likely never be seen in the public again, and that all that inheritance would be used to pay for medical bills rather than spent on whatever lavish life she'd originally planned for it.

"You actually liked Henry, didn't you?" Louis asked, causing her to glance up at him.

"He wasn't what I'd expected." She said, placing her cup down on the small platter in her other hand. "I was expecting someone like me, no care for life or love. I was surprised to find the opposite. There is something that can be appreciated in the passion of others, something to be learned from it." She stated, taking another sip from her cup.

"You could just say yes… but I believe I understand what you mean. Indeed — Henry was more broken than he was evil. Unfortunately we're the only ones that will have ever seen that in him." He stated, but blinked when J'ai chuckled and shook her head.

"No. I believe Mr. Briggs saw that as well." She saw the questioning look on Louis' face and she turned, grabbing an envelope from her desk and handing it to him. "He sent me a small letter of thanks." She said as Louis opened it. "He has also paid for a new burial site for his son, he and Henry will be buried together." Louis lowered the letter and looked down at J'ai. "A small step, but I'm sure as he said in his letter, it would be what Samuel would have wanted in the end." She would stand then and snatch the letter from Louis' hands and place it in her breast pocket. "Little too late in the end though — a gesture neither of them can appreciate."

He shook his head and followed behind her, in the end she just couldn't accept a kind gesture and genuine change. Two things she didn't believe in — there was always a motive, and this was likely no different to her. At the same time though, he believed it was just a personal wall, and over time that wall would crumble. They had eternity now, before he believed it hopeless, and yet now it seemed more likely as time went on. Like rocks on the shore, with enough time and patience even the roughest stone can be smoothed and polished. No one else might believe in her ability to change or to show kindness, but he has seen it many times from her. She has her own way of doing things, and can be cruel in her methods, but she is indeed capable.

"Well, either way I'm sure they're happy now." Louis stated as he followed behind her, closing the door of the study as they entered the hallway.

"Hm." Was all J'ai responded with. He knew how she felt about talk of an afterlife. "One can hope." He was surprised by that, no cold statement, just letting it go for once.

What happened with Samuel and his family was nothing

unusual, families disown their children for much less. What made it stand out was the length at which his own sister went to use this fact against not only her brother, but her father and his lover as well. The true monster of this story was never Henry, in the end it was Matilda and her greed. Her desire to better her own life by any means and thus throwing her family in the flames, thinking she could bridge herself across with what remained. In the end she lived, and she was truthful about seeing J'ai, but the idea that the trauma caused her to believe that was more easily acceptable given Henry denied she'd been there at all.

Matilda Briggs now sits silently in a hospital ward, paid for by the inheritance of her brother alone, though still not enough to cover the full cost of care or even prolonged care. The sobbing woman of ward ten, who receives no visitors and no letters. To J'ai this was justice enough. Even Henry said that killing her would change nothing, but that he could at least make her suffer by taking away from her the one thing he'd been so deluded into thinking he was giving to the world, her beauty.

Yes, to J'ai... that was justice.

Chapter Ten

"He just burst into the Prim, screaming about some strange door." She hummed softly. "Said he worked in the museum for five years, never saw the door before... are you listening, J'ai?" Wilhelm grumbled, turning towards the woman with folded arms.

"Hm? Oh, yes. Sorry, I was just observing him." She pointed to the man behind the glass. "Has he been doing that since he was put in that room?" She asked, side-eyeing the Inspector then.

The man sat cradled in the corner of the room with his face pressed into the corner whispering to himself. From the sound of it the same series of words over and over again — something had traumatized this man to the point of erratic behavior. Wilhelm started dribbling on again, but she heard none of it. She turned away from the one-way mirror and made for the door, stepping through it she allowed it to close slowly behind her. Wilhelm was close behind her, telling her to wait but she would obviously have none of it.

She entered the room and the mutterings became discernible. "*If I can't see them, they can't see me. If I can't see them, they can't see me.*"

She narrowed her eyes at him then turned to Wilhelm while maintaining a gesture on the babbling man. "Has he said anything else beyond that sentence?" She asked, and Wilhelm simply shook his head. "This is stranger than the Queen's letter had let on." She added, rubbing her chin thoughtfully. "Has this man had any medical attention?" She asked, not caring that they were in the same room as the 'victim'.

"No, but not for lack of trying. He wouldn't let a nurse or

doctor near him, he went mad at the sight of the needles."
Goddard stated, crossing his arms once more.

"Name?" She turned to look down at the man once more.

"Hasn't said anything other than what he is now, and we
didn't find anything on him to tell us who he is." He tossed
his hands up then allowed them to fall to his sides. "Like he
fell out of the bloody sky." He added with an annoyed
grunt.

She took a few steps forward, then knelt down next to the
man. She listened to the sentence he spoke, the repetition
in his voice, and the way his body trembled. He had gone
through something so traumatic that it left him in this state.
There was no report of anyone going missing in the last
week, however she still didn't know how many cases like
this have sprang up. She stood and turned again to
Wilhelm, motioning towards the door so they could once
again speak privately. He followed her out, being sure to
close the door as gently as he could. The poor man was
clearly through enough trauma this day.

"He behaves as though he's been tortured for months,
years even. I've seen war prisoners with those kinds of
signs of trauma – my father treated many in his career
growing up." She would turn to Wilhelm fully. "How many
cases have come through like this that the Prim has
ignored?" She was blunt in her questioning.

"None!" Wilhelm stated with an almost offended tone. "This
man is the first to stumble through our doors. We contacted
you because we didn't know who else to talk to... how was I
to know you were going to receive word from the Queen
about similar cases?" He asked, almost yelling as he
waved his arms angrily.

"I find that hard to believe – I don't especially believe in coincidences, Wilhelm. If not here then have you heard of anything similar happening anywhere else?" She asked, and for a moment he pondered.

"Nothin' directly…" He spoke, a bit of the old slang hitting his tone. "Well… maybe. It's a little personal though." He admitted rubbing the back of his neck in a shy manner.

"Mel?" She asked, crossing her arms curiously.

"No, you don't get to call my fiance Mel." He said pointing at her.

"Fine, Melody." She shook her head. "What a name for a child…" She muttered softly.

"Not Mel directly, but her mother. She is being taken care of by her father, something happened to her mother. Scared her so bad she can't have a mirror anywhere in her room or she goes mad." He shook his head.

"That isn't a reported incident though…" J'ai stated, rubbing her chin thoughtfully. "Perhaps this is something that people don't normally escape from." She said, turning then to look to Wilhelm once more. "I'm going to talk to him – stay out here." He was about to speak but she stopped him. "Go into your observation room – I know you *have* to watch." She huffed and pulled the door open, the man whimpering and covering his head as she moved across the room and to him before the door even clicked shut again.

She stood idly over him for a long moment with her hands cupped behind her back, tilting her head as she observed him and watched him tremble in this corner. She'd seen children tremble in this fashion in homes, hospitals, and even right here in the rooms of Primburogh, but rarely grown men – perhaps women, but very rarely this. She knelt down next to the man, reaching out she placed a hand on the man's back – he tensed under her touch and she hummed curiously realizing then just how tightly he was pressed into the wall, like he willed himself to become the very wall itself.

"Sir, my name is J'ai Mauvais. I'm working with the royal family to investigate what happened to you." He didn't seem to hear. "What is your name?" She asked, but got no answer. "Do you have people we could get in contact with?" His entire body froze, and his head slowly lifted. "A wife? Child perhaps?" She continued on that topic.

"My son…" He whispered softly. "My son." He repeated, body shaking again.

"Where is your son? Where do you live, or where does your son live?" He placed his hand on the wall and slowly looked up. She followed his gaze, but dropped it since there was nothing visible there. "Sir I can't help you if you do-" She was cut off when he turned and gripped her shoulders.

"My son was with me, he was there, he was still there!" He exclaimed, beginning to sob. She stared at him, her own hands gripping his wrists to maintain some control. "He can't stay there, you have to get him back!" He was shaking again, and his sobbing intensified. "Please, he's just a boy! Please." He begged, and J'ai sighed softly.

"I won't promise anything, but first I need to know more about what happened to you. You have to tell me everything." She said, watching as he slowly tried to collect himself. Not for himself but for this boy of his.

"It was… normal. A normal evening. I work the night shift at the fishery, my son and I just patrol the factory and make sure nothing happens since drunks like to sneak in some nights to sleep." He paused, seemingly thinking about that night. "We went to the basement of the factory because the boss usually hide a bottle of rum down there, and I figured my boy and I could bond over our first drink... we had a drink or two from the bosses stash and walked around the basement chatting for a bit and that is when we noticed it – the door." He pressed his back deeper into the corner. "It was strangely clean and white, not a door you'd see in a factory, it was like a house door but a rich house... I've been in that factory for years... I've never seen that door in my life. It was that door that changed everything." Tears began to fall down his cheeks again. "Curiosity drove me to walk myself and my son through that door."

There was an eerie silence that lingered through the factory; the rain pattered against the tall windows that echoed softly through the building, adding to the ambiance around the seemingly abandoned building. The door at the front of the building creaked with a metallic screech, the metal of the door dragging sharply against the floor as the two stepped inside. His name was Peter, only in his mid thirties with a loving wife and their only son, Jack. Peter worked as a night-watch for the factory for ten years, and tonight was Jack's first night working with his father. He hoped it would go well, and soon his son could help provide for their growing family as his wife was once preparing for their second child.

"Now remember Jack, keep your lantern up, and be sure to check corners. Drunks like to crawl into the crevices, and the boss won't be happy if there are hungover bastards on their property." He said and smiled as his son nodded and did as he was told as he lit his own lantern. "You walk along the left side of the building and I'll take the right. We'll meet at the end alright?" He asked and again the boy nodded quickly.

The two parted ways and started making their rounds. The light from his lantern slowly brightened any dark corner, like milk spilling over a table. The lantern's light reached out in all directions slowly engulfing everything around it, only to be swallowed by the darkness that grew back behind Peter. He glanced over to the other side of the building and saw his son making slow progress as he checked every corner. He smiled, proud of his son and proud of his eagerness to help prepare for his little brother or sister's arrival. It took a little longer than normal for the round to be finished as he waited at the end of the hall for his son, who would finally rush up to him as he made a pass around the last corner.

"Anything worth noting?" He would ask, watching little Jack switch hands with his lantern.

"Nothing father, not a drunk that I saw." He said smiling ear to ear then, proud of himself.

"Good. Now we move downstairs." He said, turning to shine his lantern down the blackened steps behind them. He felt Jack move closer to him, and he chuckled. "You'll have to get used to this kind of darkness, boy. Now go on, take the lead." He said, nodding his head forward as a signal for his son to go.

Jack swallowed back a lump and moved forward. He lifted his lantern and took a shaky step forward, glancing back to make sure his father was still behind him. Peter smiled down at his son, and almost laughed when the boy gave him a worried smile in return before turning his gaze forward once more. They went through each room below the factory, finally coming to a stop in front of the manager's office. Peter would grin and put a hand on his son's shoulder and motioned toward the door, the two slowly stepping inside and closing the door behind them. Jack watched his father walk around the room before kneeling down and reaching under the oak desk at the back of the room, producing a half-full bottle of rum.

"You did good, son." He said walking back to the boy. "You're a man now, a working man at that. It's only right that a father should share a drink with his son in these moments." He said uncorking the bottle and taking a swig before passing it down to Jack.

"What about mom?" He asked slowly, taking the bottle into his hands. "Won't she be mad?" He added sniffing the substance.

"What mother doesn't know couldn't harm her." Peter stated and ruffled his son's hair.

The two shared a couple drinks and more than a couple laughs that night. They sat in the manager's office for some time before the muffled sound of the bell echoed through the building to them. Peter smiled and put the bottle back where he'd found it and told his son it was time to clock out. They would do one more sweep as they walked out of the building, but before they could even do that secondary sweep they would stop as they exited the manager's office. The two would stand still as stone as they just stared forward for a long moment, a clear look of confusion on both of their faces.

"Dad…" Jack spoke softly as he reached up and grabbed his father's arm.

"I see…" Peter replied, taking a step forward. He reached his hand out, before them was a door that he'd never seen before. A white door, like it had only just been installed here, but neither of them heard anyone – beyond even that was the impossibility of such a thing happening right under their noses. He looked down to the clean handle of the door and slowly reached for it, only to stop when he felt his son grip his forearm.

"Dad, let's go home." He whispered, but Peter only smiled.

"We have to check every room Jack, remember?" He asked and after a moment of hesitation his son nodded his head.

He gripped the handle and slowly pushed it open, a light brighter than any he'd seen filtering out and slowly enveloping them as the door opened fully. So bright he had to shield his own eyes, the two dropping their lanterns in the process of trying to protect their vision. After what felt like hours, Peter would finally lower his arms, adjusting to the brightness of this place he looked around, and then down to the boy hiding his face into his side. He placed a hand on his son's back and took in everything this room, this place had to offer. It was a strangely large room, open but with many walls all around them that had hallways that seemed to lead nowhere.

"A...maze?" Peter questioned under his breath.

"Dad!" He turned, looking down to his son then.

The boy pointed behind them, his eyes following his son's finger back in the direction they had come, his eyes widening as he looked at the barren wall behind them. He took a staggered step forward and placed his hands on the wall where the door had been only moments ago. He heard his son begin to sob quietly behind him as he continued to run his hands over the wall, his own silent panic enveloping him in that moment, but he had to hide it – if not for his own sake than for his son's. He would turn and kneel down in front of the boy, pulling him in to comfort him. A man by title maybe, but he was still just a boy to Peter. He had to protect his son, even if it was from his own emotions.

"Dad… where are we?" Jack asked, clinging to his father.

"… I don't know." He would look around, looking down a hallway that seemed to go on longer than all the others. "Come on, let's go this way and see if the way out is there." He said, standing and walking with his son's hand in his own, but there was firm hesitation in the boy's steps.

"What if… there isn't?" He asked, his voice trembling as he spoke.

"Then we keep looking. Understand?" He asked, and again knelt down in front of him. "We have to get back to mom. Remember what I told you?" He asked, placing his hand on his son's cheek.

"We're the men of the house. Mom needs us – mom and the baby need us." He said, but the fear was still in his voice. "I remember." He added, nodding his head then.

"We have to for mom. Just keep telling yourself that, Jack." Peter stated then stood.

The two walked forward down the long hallway – the light seemed to follow them almost. The deeper they went down the hall, the darker it became behind them. In a way it reminded Jack of the way the light of the lantern filtered through the factory, enveloping everything in front with light but obscuring everything behind them in shadows. He stayed as close as he could to his father, repeating what he had said over and over in his own head. Mom needed them – they had to get home – dad would get us out. He believed in his father, believed he would lead them right out of this weird place – this nightmare. Maybe that's all this was, a nightmare he was having. Maybe he'd just fallen asleep after those couple drinks with his father – they did make him feel very warm, and like he was swimming without water.

"Jack." His father's voice caused him to freeze. "Be quiet… listen." He turned his eyes forward and from the darkness ahead a low rumbling echoed back, like a feral hound in the night but *more*. "Back up." His father stated, pushing him back. "Go… go." His father turned and pushed him back.

There was a loud, shrill growl followed by the sound of something moving behind them, growing closer. Peter dared to glance behind them and his eyes widened, skin went white as a sheet of ice. He pushed his son, calling for him to run, and run Jack did. He heard his father cry out and the sound of whatever it was behind them bellow out in rage. He closed his eyes and sprinted into the darkness running into a wall blocking the way they had come from. He turned and realized that way was not blocked as well but an opening to his left was presented. He ran, disappearing deeper into this nightmare maze, and the sound of his father's screams fading behind him.

"So what was it?" J'ai asked, still standing above Peter as he recounted the nightmarish tale.

"… I don't know – it was nothing I've ever seen or heard of. It was like a shadow, but I felt it. I heard it." He choked back a sob.

"How did you escape it?" She asked, crossing her arms over her chest as she thought for a moment.

"I turned over, covered my head to stop it from hurting me… then it just… started running in the direction Jack went and I…" He paused. A look in his eye like he'd gone back to that place in his mind. "I called out to Jack, told him not to look at them… it's the only thing I could think of that made it go away… it sounds silly but… it was like a… a"

"A monster from a child's dream." J'ai spoke softly, then quickly turned to the door.

"Wait!" He called, reaching out to her in that moment. "You'll find him won't you? My son, my Jack..." Tears poured down his cheeks.

"I already told you. I promise nothing... but I will do my best." She said, opening the door and stepping outside.

Wilhelm was waiting for her in the hall – she walked past him, but he reached out and took her by the wrist causing her to turn back and glare at him. Slowly he released her wrist, and cleared his throat – he had realized he overstepped a boundary with her in that moment. Her glare continued to eat through him, asking him what he wanted without even saying it, but he couldn't bring himself to speak right away.

"... Peter... he spoke to you. You believe all of that, what he said?" He asked, and J'ai scoffed.

"I do." She answered simply.

"How? It's such an outlandish story. Perhaps he got drunk and... something happened with him and his boy and now he's just—" She put a hand up to stop his senseless dribble in that moment.

"Willy... look at me." She said, and for a moment he did look her up and down, then shrugged. "I will live forever – never die, and never grow old. You watched me be hanged, burned at the stake, and placed before a firing squad." They stared at one another for a long moment before he cleared his throat once more, shoving his hands into his pockets.

"You have a fair point, but doors leading into unending mazes with monsters… that's… insanity." Wilhelm stated once more. "I understand your point, but this is something completely…" He struggled to find the word.

"Fascinating." She finished his sentence for him as she turned and continued down the hall, the Inspector close behind. "Louis has slept the day away enough, it's time to work." She said pushing the doors to the Bully-pen open so that she could once more be out in the dreary open air of Victoria.

"I'm surprised you allow Louis to sleep in. You two are practically joined at the hip." Wilhelm stated, a slight jealousy lacing his tone.

"Louis has a life beyond being my butler and guard." She smirked as she stepped up to the carriage. "It was the least I could do for him, he had quite the long night." She stated, making no effort to elaborate on her statement.

"A date? Louis? He doesn't seem the type to be chasing ladies." He said, suddenly interested. "Who was this lucky lady, eh? You know don't you? You always know." J'ai said nothing, simply turned her gaze out the window. "You should take a note from Louis – while neither of you will grow old that doesn't mean neither of you can love." He stated, crossing his arms as he leaned back in his seat.

"I have no time for *love*." She stated, never once tearing her gaze from the window. "Louis can be as selfish as he pleases, but I'll not put such pain on someone so dear to me." She said, waving her hand idly to clear the subject. "We'll have to go to that factory, if that's where the door appeared for Peter then perhaps we can make it show itself again for us." She changed the subject back to that of work.

Wilhelm eyed her for a long moment – she viewed love as something selfish. Why? Because of her immortality? He still didn't understand how this all happened to her – she always changed the topic or ignored it altogether whenever he would even start hinting towards it. He sighed and turned his own gaze out the window as well. He thought of Peter – his story about the room, that door. Doors lined the streets, each one leading into someone's home or a place of business. He never thought that maybe one of those doors – perhaps more than one – could lead to a place of nightmares where some seemingly never escape. He shuddered at the thought of such a place – his mind unable to grasp the very idea of it and yet, J'ai seemed to embrace it right away.

"Like monsters from a child's dream..."

Chapter Eleven

"Dad... ?"

Jack's voice spoke out in a trembled whisper as he slowly walked along this never-ending hallway. He'd been following the same path since he'd gotten separated from his father. This hall was different from the last one though – it was brightly lit, and the floor was carpeted in a way that he'd imagined the Queen's palace to be decorated. The walls were white and barren – plain – it made this place feel empty and uneasy to one's soul. The obvious emptiness as well added to the uneasy energy this strange place gave off, and all he could think about was his desire to go home.

The soft sounds of him beginning to sob would fill the space around him as he sank to the floor. "I... want my mum." He whimpered as he curled up onto his side.

This odd moment of peace granted him a moment to process his feelings, to allow fear into his heart and the realization that he might never get out of this place to sink in. He cried, like a child he would weep for what felt like forever, his hands clasped over his mouth to muffle his sobs out of fear of something – *anything* hearing him in this moment. A breeze would fill the hall suddenly, like the cold air of fall washing over him causing him to pause. It was the same sensation of a carriage passing you on the street, the gust of wind as something moves by you at a quicker pace than your own.

He shifted and looked around him – the light in the room had grown dim, and the wall paper had begun to peel. Like several decades had passed in the moments he'd been crying, but within the dim light that lingered there was a brighter light at the end of the hall. He stood and slowly walked towards it on trembling feet, coming to a slow halt just before it. A door, similar to the one that had brought him and his father here. His heart leapt for joy as he sprung forward, taking the knob into his hand, and ready at any moment to fling it wide open and return home. Then he thought of his father – he was still here somewhere… or maybe that thing killed him. His fingers grew cold – he pulled his hand away from the door and stood there rubbing his hands together nervously.

He'd not thought of it until now, the idea that his father could be dead. What would he tell his mother? How could he explain this? No one would believe him – no one could believe a story like this. Then there was the possibility that his father was alive – he couldn't just leave him here, could he? The sting of the cold in his fingertips caused his heart rate to rise – his hands always went cold when he was upset, or scared, and right now he was absolutely terrified. He sniffled, and when he did he noticed something new: a smell. Like bad eggs, but somehow worse. A low rumble came from somewhere behind him, like the intense growling of a mad dog, and in that moment the hairs on the back of Jack's neck stood.

Slowly he turned around, his trembling gaze turning back towards the way he'd come. The dim light that once lit the hall had now gone completely black, and in the far distance he saw the glaring yellow eyes looking back at him. He saw nothing else in the blackness of the room, only the gaze, and in that moment he turned back to the door and moved forward only to find the door was gone. The sound of the monster growing closer caused him to shake – he didn't know what to do. He began to cry, throwing his arms over his head and sinking to the floor, his face towards the wall as he begged for his mother or his father, anyone at all to save him.

I don't want to die!

The only thought running through his head as he felt the

vibration on the floor as the beast stood right behind him. He went still like a fawn in tall grass, listening to the sounds that came from the creature behind him. It's breath was heavy and aggressive, each exhale was accompanied by a deep growl that seemed to ripple through its lungs. Then his body tensed once more as he felt something press into his back, and then the sensation of his shirt shifting over his skin as this thing sniffed his body. He wanted to scream and cry – run away – anything at all to get away in that moment but his legs refused to listen, refused to budge. The beast let out another growl, and then he listened to the sound of it's heavy steps shuffle and fade into the distance.

He stayed like that – he wasn't sure for how long, but he remained pressed into the wall as though it were the only thing keeping him safe in that moment. Finally however he would dare to peek around him to see the room was alight again, and the walls were the same peaceful, plain white they were when he'd first started walking down this hall. He felt alone again, and his whole body began to shake as he finally looked around the room. Yes, the long hallway had changed again, and now it had become much wider with a single hallway that narrowed out and stretched into the darkness as with all the others, but he had more choices this time. The room he sat in had changed as well, beyond just a hallway that seemed to take him back the way he'd come, and likely would lead him right into the path of whatever this creature was that lived in this place, but more than that each side of the room was lined with eight doors – sixteen in total doors for him to choose from – all looked exactly the same.

"No!" He screamed and burst to his feet. "Dad! Dad!!" He called out as he ran towards the hallway. "Dad – where are you!?" His voice faded as he disappeared into the darkness that swallowed him.

The light would slowly fade from the room, different than if the sun were setting or if a candle was fading. Instead it seemed like the light was beginning to melt away the farther from this part of the room he went, until nothing remained but inky darkness. Slowly nine, blinking yellow eyes formed in the darkness, the sound of the boy's screaming barely audible now. It would follow though – it always followed, and in its wake it aged and destroyed all that was around it – the wall paper curling as it drew closer, and the smell lingered in the air. Another hall would present itself to the boy being followed by shadow, a never ending maze of winding, ever changing hallways and rooms. Its hunting ground – its spider's web.

"Jack!" He stopped and listened. *"Jack! Where are you?!"*

"Dad?!" He called back to the voice and waited, staring for a long time down the newly presented hallway.

"This way, Jack!"

He hesitated for a moment, the voice was so far away he wasn't sure if it sounded like his father or not, but the person knew his name. He took in a breath and started running down the hall and into the darkness. It enveloped him – there was no light to guide him like all the other times, and he had to slow down and put his hand on the wall next to him to be sure he was still going down the right path. He listened to every little sound, listening not only for the voice that had called out to him, but for whatever it was that had approached him in that room before. The desire to go home was still a strong one, but the desire to find his father was even stronger – men don't leave their family behind.

"Dad… where are you?" He whispered out, too afraid to speak any louder.

"This way Jack…"

The voice came from another hall, dimly lit but still brighter than this hall. He could smell it, but his dad was the only thing he could think about as he stepped into the hallway. The light flickered like dying candles all around him as he slowly moved forward. He tried to muster the courage to call for his father again, but couldn't. Something was wrong, he could feel it – like an ache in his stomach that rose to his chest. His fingers were cold again, and idly he rubbed his hands as he walked forward. That familiar gust of air hit him again, but this time it was like ice right against the back of his neck. Against his better judgment he slowly turned around, coming face to face with those nine yellow eyes.

It was quick – in an instant something black, and sticky was clinging to him. He screamed, and struggled as he fell to the floor trying to get whatever it was off his face, but it was no use. Once it had a hold on something living, that thing belonged to the shadow from that moment onward. He gagged as it's inky body forced its way into his mouth and down his throat. He choked as his eyes rolled into the back of his head, his body seizing on the ground violently, practically slamming into the surface beneath him before coming to a more sudden stop. Silence lingered, and slowly the lights returned to the constant dim light. He sat up, his eyes staring forward blankly before he would slowly rise to his feet and regain his balance.

He looked around the room for a moment, taking everything in like he was searching for something. Suddenly he would stop, and face the far wall, slowly approaching it. He would tilt his head slowly to the left before reaching out and tearing the wallpaper away revealing a door beneath the surface. Without hesitation he would reach out and open the door, a warm light filling the room around him as he stared into the doorway. He would smile, a line of drool leaking down his chin, his throat bulged and his mouth was forced open as a sickly yellow eye peered from within Jack's mouth.

"FREEDOM..."

Chapter Twelve

"We had the factory shut down – we're treating it as though someone ran off with the boy." Wilhelm spoke as the carriage rolled up next to the factory. "It's the first time those stacks aren't spitting smoke." He added with a soft exhale.

"Probably for the best." J'ai stated, reaching for the carriage door.

"Even one day of work lost for these men is a meal lost. A lot of people rely on this place for-" He stopped when he noticed the dry annoyance in J'ai's eyes.

"Not the factory, idiot, the kidnapping story." She said, and for a moment he stared back at her in shock. "Don't let it go to your head."

"Was that meant to be a compliment?" They practically spoke over each other.

"I said don't let it go to your head. It was a good decision, because it's clear this goes beyond a simple murder or kidnapping by the normal definition of the words as we know them." She said pushing the door open and stepping out, taking away the chance for him to reply to her.

He would smirk though, it'd been months since she'd been arrested, and three months more since the Doll-maker case. She had assisted in one other case before this, a fairly simple one involving a missing man that ultimately turned out to be a case of a husband running off from his family duties to be with another woman. Cut and dry really, in her words. As they walked towards the factory he took note of the group of workers loitering beyond the line, while his men stood idly in case anyone from the groups decided they were going in regardless. He stared up at the building then as the high cylinder stacks shadowed over them the closer to the door they got, the cracked and faded bricks that held the structure in place seemingly staring back at them the closer they got.

"Dad..."

J'ai stopped, causing him to stop just behind her. All eyes watched the wide open double doors of the factory, watching the shadows within. The sun stopped just at the entrance – suddenly a pair of worn children's work shoes stepped into the open, and young Jack winced as the sun hit his face. Instinctively he shielded his eyes, then looked to all the faces staring back at him – there was a long moment of silence as he examined each and every face before coming to a stop on J'ai's face. He noted the clear look of confusion as she stared at him, and almost like a switch the boy would drop to his knees and begin to sob, crying out for his father in that moment. Wilhelm pushed past her along with two other patrolmen who immediately began to comfort the boy.

She would move forward finally and look down at the boy. He sobbed, and sniffled while Wilhelm took off his coat and draped it over the boy's shoulders. She arched a brow taking in the look of the lad before her – messy brown hair, similar but slightly lighter. Pale skin stained with a bit of dirt from a hard life – maybe from spending the night on a factory floor, but the more she looked the more this whole scene appeared odd. His father was traumatized, nearly beyond speaking, and here this boy was sobbing before everyone, and yet not a single tear stained his cheeks. The sounds were there, but the effect only did so much without actual tears, and on top of that he didn't seem to be at all trembling.
"Wilhelm..." She reached out to touch his shoulder – he looked up at her. "Come with me, please." She said and stepped away from him and the boy then and partly inside

the factory itself.

"Right… you!" He pointed to one of the patrol officers. "Get this boy a carriage and wait for me." He ordered and the man nodded before jogging off to complete his task. "Wait right here, son." He added ruffling the boy's hair before rising to his feet and making his way towards J'ai. "What is it?" He asked, crossing his arms as he took note of the oddly thoughtful look she had.

"You're taking him back to the Prim?" She asked, and he nodded quickly. "Do that… but keep him separate from his father until I get there." She said, and now it was Wilhelm's turn to look confused.

"Why? The poor boy is crying for his father as we speak." He said motioning to the boy curled up not far behind them.

"I want to look around the factory, but I also want to talk to the boy before he gets put back with his father. If he's with his father there is a high chance he won't be willing to speak to me, or his father won't be willing to allow me to speak to him. Please, put the boy in a separate room and just keep an eye on him okay?" She asked, and Wilhelm rolled his eyes and finally nodded.

"Yes, fine. Am I at least allowed to tell the poor man his boy is okay?" He asked, clearly getting annoyed with her over this.

"No. Don't say a word to him." She said, her eyes staring past Wilhelm to see Jack watching them out of the corner of his eye, and then look away when the patrolman from before approached him. "Something strange is happening here – give me an hour to have a look around. Oh-" She would add, halfway turned around before looking back. "Could you have one of your patrols run to my manor and fetch Louis for me? Unfortunately I may need him after all."

She added as he watched her move deeper into the factory.

He turned around and saw the boy was gone, and assumed the patrolman had taken him to the carriage. Wilhelm would make his way back through the crowd that had now grown in numbers as people passing by became curious about the happenings here. He moved up to the carriage and opened the door with a soft click – the boy, Jack, was slumped over on the seat fast asleep. The sight brought a gentle smile to his lips as he lifted the lad's head and slipped into the seat, trying his best not to disturb the boy's slumber. The patrolman sat still as stone, staring blankly towards Wilhelm when their eyes locked.

"I'll take the boy inside the Prim when we arrive – I have another task for you, Will." He said, and the man tilted his head slightly.

"What task, sir?" He asked, the tone of his voice was strange, almost indifferent in that moment.

"I… need you to stop at Madam Mauvais' manor and fetch her butler, Louis." He said, glancing down at the boy as the carriage began to move towards Primburogh. "Escort him to the Prim, of course, and get him up to date on what you know and I'm sure J'ai will fill in the rest of the blanks." He said waving his hand passively.

"Yes sir." Will answered quickly.

The sun peeked through the window of the manor's guest room – it stretched across the wooden floor and over the end of the bed. The blankets draped messily over the edge, Louis slept barely covered beneath them. The door creaked open softly and Caroline quietly stepped in, and smiled when she looked to see Louis still fast asleep. Closing the door behind her with a bump from her hip, she would approach the bed with a tray of lunch for him. She placed the tray down on the night stand near the bed and turned towards the bed, before leaning over him and planting a soft kiss on his cheek.

"Good morning." She would chuckle as he shifted beneath her. "Well good afternoon I mean." She would correct herself as he twisted around onto his back and sat up with a grunt. "Sleep well?" She asked, grabbing the tray and placing it in his lap.

"Better than usual." He answered, taking a slice of toast and taking a bite from it. "You?" He would ask then. "I hope I didn't move around too much." He said, smirking as she blushed slightly.

"I slept just fine, thank you." She answered sitting on the edge of the bed and crossing her arms.

"I'm glad, usually I toss and turn. I was worried it would disturb you." He said before taking a drink of his tea.

There was a long pause between them as she fiddled with the straps of her apron. "Louis..." She said his name – he hummed a questioning response. "What are we?" She asked, noting the sudden silence that came from him. She imagined him just staring at the back of her head, dumbfounded. "I'm sorry, ignore me. Just the maid and her prattling–" She gasped when she felt his arm fold around her from behind. "Louis—" He would shush her softly.

"You're not *just a maid*. You are an intelligent, beautiful woman." He would lean over her shoulder and smile as he kissed her softly on the cheek. "Of course I love you, Caroline." His tone was assuring.

Her cheeks remained tinted as she looked at him, a smile

creeping softly over her expression. He leaned in and kissed her, and she melted right into him in that moment, wrapping her arms around his neck. They were close to having another moment to themselves when a loud bell rang from downstairs – she pulled away and looked towards her bedroom door. She would let out a breathy chuckle and slip from the bed, smiling when she saw him slump his head and turn with a shrug.

"Get dressed, I'm sure the Madam is getting impatient." She said, and paused only briefly when Louis laughed.

"Perhaps... then again she was the one that gave me the day off." He said, but then stood from the bed so that he could get dressed. "You're right though, I'm sure she's tired of having Wilhelm as a replacement." He added with another laugh.

She moved quickly down the stairs as the bell was told once more – she called out to let the person know she was coming. She smoothed out her apron, and quickly fixed her hair before pulling the door open. She was greeted by the patrolman, who bent his head in greeting then slowly glanced around the room behind her. She stared at him for a long time, his eyes slowly coming back to meet hers, and without a word she took a step back.

"Is a man named Louis here?" He asked, taking a step over the threshold.

"He's upstairs getting ready." She answered, suddenly trying to avoid looking at the man.

"May I wait inside?" He asked, narrowing his eyes as he looked at her.

She nodded and quickly closed the door as he stepped the rest of the way in. She made for the stairs, assuming he would understand that she was going to fetch Louis. She would look back at him, feeling the shudder travel down her spine as his eyes remained locked onto her as she disappeared down the hall at the top of the stairs. She exhaled a sharp breath and leaned against the wall, to calm her nerves as she had begun to shake the moment she was far enough away from him. She had always had what her mother called "the sight" – she could see people for what they were and understand their true intentions, for the most part. The only one she couldn't fully read was J'ai, and in the beginning Louis before he finally opened up to her… but this man – this patrolman.

Black. All she saw was black-like smoke billowing off him. The tint of yellow barely visible at the very edge of the aura that masked this man downstairs. She'd not seen anything like that since she was a girl – since her mother disappeared. The memories were buried deep within her, all she remembered was her mother telling her to cover her eyes to the shadow, and then nothing beyond that. She exhaled another breath and quickly made her way to her room, opening the door and closing it behind her. Louis was fixing his sleeves when he turned to look at her, his expression becoming concerned at how pale she seemed.

"Are you—" He was cut off.

"I'm fine. There is a patrolman downstairs." He looked towards the door. "Louis…" She took his arm desperately in her hands. "Don't go with him." She pleaded looking up to him.

He was about to question her when the door bowed inward then exploded into pieces – Louis wrapped his arms around her letting the pieces bounce off his back before turning around to see the patrolman standing in the doorway. His arm bulged and ripped from his uniform as a thick, dripping black appendage gripped the edge of the doorway, and pulled the patrolman into the room. His left eye rolled into the back of his head turning a sickly yellow before a red iris appeared in the center and focused in on Louis.

"New host." The eye flicked to Caroline. "Enemy."

Louis pushed Caroline back onto the bed and grabbed a blade from beneath his pillow. "As soon as there is an opening you run. Find J'ai." He told her and she nodded.

"Surrender." The patrolman said sternly, watching as Louis approached him.

"Not hardly." Louis replied as he twisted the blade in his hand.

"Then... die." His arm whipped out and wrapped around Louis' throat and tossed him to the side of the room.

Caroline screamed as she watched him crash against the wall and slide down. The patrolman moved from the door and approached Louis – Caroline took that chance to rush to the door but was stopped as that tendril wrapped around her own throat and began to squeeze, the sound of her muscles crunching under the limb as she was lifted from the ground. Louis rose from the rubble of a broken dresser and looked up to see him holding her up in the air. He growled and rushed him, shoving the blade into the man. A wild shriek echoed from the mouth of the patrolman as he dropped the woman and slammed the tendril into Louis, pushing him against the wall.

"Caroline! Go!" He yelled at her – she looked up from the floor, a hand clasped to her neck. "Go now!" He yelled again.

She hesitated for only a second before lifting her dress and rushing down the hall – she stumbled and almost fell down the stairs, but caught herself on the banister. The sunlight greeted her and she rushed out – down the long pathway towards the gate that bordered the property and led into town. She froze only when she heard the sound of glass shattering, and turned to see Louis being tossed around the room like a doll. He would be okay – that was the thought that filtered through her mind. She knew he would be okay, but she had to hurry to Primburogh – the only place she could think the Madam would be. She removed her shoes and tied her dress up so that it didn't get in her way as she began to run along the pathway – hopefully towards help.

Chapter Thirteen

The boy slept soundly in the interrogation room – Wilhelm stood behind the one-way window with a look of thoughtful confusion as he stood there. Time had ticked on and J'ai had yet to turn up and still Louis hadn't arrived either. He turned his eyes to the clock on the wall, and furrowed his brows – his attention was pulled back when he saw the boy stirring. He moved and quickly made his way inside the room, the boy sitting up and looking all around him. A reflection of fear and confusion was in his gaze as Wilhelm entered the room. He jumped from his seat and tripped backwards, sliding back into the wall where he would hide his face from the older man that now entered the room.

"Easy there, son… you've been asleep for some time." He said, moving one of the chairs from the interrogation table so that he could sit near the boy.

"W-where…?" It was the only word he could muster to say at this moment. "This… is another trick." He whispered to himself, and Wilhelm's brows furrowed in confusion.

"Trick? This isn't a trick I can assure you." He said, reaching out then to place a hand on the boy's shoulder.

"NO!!" He screamed out, and turning around suddenly the boy would latch his teeth into Wilhelm's hand, causing him to curse.

Other officers came into the room then, and subdued the boy. The entire time the other officers tried to restrain the boy he screamed and kicked, a look of anger and fear contorting the boy's features. Wilhelm stood with his hand gripped in his uninjured one before he would finally look down, and see the blood dripping from his skin. Something wasn't right, this isn't how he was before. He turned and made his way out the door, his officers calling to him as he grabbed his coat and walked out of the building. He called out for a passing carriage and climbed into the back – the driver pushed open the small dividing window behind where he sat and peered inside at Wilhelm.

"To the Fishery, as fast as you can go, sir. I'll be sure to pay double for your troubles." Wilhelm stated, and with a simple nod of confirmation the driver motivated his horse to turn around and head for the factory on the double, as his customer ordered.

He sat with his arms crossed over his chest as buildings rushed by him, his leg jostled impatiently as he thought for a moment about what had happened. That boy wasn't like that when he walked out of that building, and he goes back to the Prim and wakes up in a horror like he was. J'ai saw it, that was why she insisted they separate the son from his father, but then what the hell happened in the short trip from the factory to Primburogh? It wasn't making any sense. The carriage came to a sudden halt, and then he heard the driver cry out angrily – Wilhelm leaned out the window to see the young maid from J'ai's manor desperately pleading for help.

"Hold on." Wilhelm spoke, trying to calm the driver down. "Caroline?" He asked and she looked over to him. She threw herself into him, and began to sob. "Calm down. What is going on?" He looked down and saw she had lost a slipper during her run. "Get inside the carriage – you can explain everything." She shook her head frantically.

"I need you to send your men to the manor!" She cried out. "A man dressed as a patrolman came to the door – "

"Yes, Will. I sent him to collect Louis as J'ai had asked of me." He said, finally coaxing her into the carriage.

"He showed up and, and..." She began to sob once more.

"He started attacking Louis – his arm got strange and his eye…" She trembled at the memory, unable to truly describe what had happened. "He tried to kill me, and Louis is still at the manor with him!" She pointed to the bruising on her neck, and the small cuts on her arms and legs.

"Caroline…" Wilhelm trailed off.

"Please! Inspector, please – Louis needs help!" She begged, placing her hands on his.

He took a moment and then sighed before leaning up and tapping on the divider. "Turn around, back to the Prim. I have to gather some of my men." He ordered and the driver nodded, once more turning around. "You're sure of what you saw?" He asked Caroline and she nodded quickly. "Fine then, once I get back and get my men together you take this carriage and find your Madam. She's at the Fishery on the West end just on the other side of the bridge." He explained and she nodded. "Tell her what is happening, she will likely know what to do." Wilhelm tried to be reassuring in that moment, but there was a feeling inside him that told him this time things were much different.

Today would not end well.

J'ai walked slowly through the factory, taking in every dark or shadowed corner the building had to offer. The scent in the factory was like the docks in summer, when the fishing boats come home and offload their catches to the highest bidders in market, or anyone with enough to offer there outright. The fishery had grown in business this past season. Walking through the building, nothing jumped out at her that proved of any interest. She made her way to the back of the factory, where that man had said they'd first encountered the door and peered into the overseer's office.

Sure enough there was an opened bottle of whiskey on the desk, enough drank from the bottle to know it had been taken advantage of the night before. She couldn't help but begin to wonder if all this wasn't just some drunken nightmare – the boy acted fine, but something just wasn't adding up at all in this situation. She stared at the bottle for a long moment before reaching out and picking up the cork, taking in the scent from it. Nothing abnormal about the whiskey – she smelled no foreign substances so poison or hallucinogens weren't the cause.

She placed the bottle back down on the table and shoved her hands into the pockets of her pants, walking back out of the room. She was about to turn for the basement when something caught her eye, and for a moment out of the corner of her gaze she saw something flickering. She turned to face the wall in front of the office door, and her eyes narrowed as she took a step forward. Reaching out she placed her hand against the rough brick surface and gently let her hand slide down the wall, half expecting some strange thing to happen in that moment but nothing did.

She turned away and started for the basement when she heard the scraping of metal. "Madam!" Caroline's voice echoed through the factory, and she turned around to see the woman running all the way from the entrance.

"Be careful! There are a lot of sharp things in here." She warned, crossing her arms as the young woman stopped in front of her.

"No time, we have to get back to the manor!" She exclaimed taking hold of J'ai's wrist, but her grasp was quickly rejected when J'ai pulled her limb free with a swift jerk.

"I have nothing but time, Caroline. What is going on?" She

looked past her and a flash of confusion came over her face. "Where is Louis?" She asked, and her eyes flicked down once more when she felt Caroline take hold of her once more.

"He's still home, fighting with some *thing* that came to our home pretending to be a patrolman!" Caroline exclaimed, and jerked J'ai forward with a much more stern grip. "We don't have time for your stupid control issues!" Caroline added and J'ai smirked.

"Interesting – so it is *something*." She glanced back, then reversed the grip on Caroline and pulled her back to the office and stood her in the hallway. "Do you see anything at all? Something strange or out of the ordinary?" Caroline looked back at her with confusion and impatience. "We'll go soon, I promise. Just… humor me." She added and Caroline sighed as she looked around the room.

Her eyes paused on the wall across from the overseer's office and she slowly stepped forward. As J'ai had done she reached out and placed her hand on the cool rough bricks. There was a darkness that lingered here – the wall to Caroline was a different shade from the other walls around It. It wasn't a huge difference and someone not used to seeing such things or the differences in colors wouldn't know what they were looking for… sometimes it's the light of the room that has this effect on some surfaces, but sometimes it's something worse.

"Something is… strange about this wall." Caroline stated, looking towards J'ai. "How–" J'ai waved her hand passively.

"I pay attention. You have a bad habit of staring for long periods of time, and I only assumed you can see things not most others can." She approached the wall and placed her hand next to Caroline's. "How was Louis the last time you saw him?" She asked suddenly, and Caroline's gaze snapped up at her. "Don't look at me that way, I may not sound it but I'm genuinely concerned." She added as she patted her hands clean.

"Then let's go! There is a carriage outside waiting." She said, making a motion with her hands so J'ai would hurry. "The Inspector and other's from the Prim are heading to the manor right now." It was only then that J'ai stopped and looked back to Caroline.

"Wilhelm is sending his men to my house? To deal with what?" She asked, then shook her head and started for the carriage.

"Wait! You'll run off at the idea of Wilhelm and the rest of Primburogh raiding your house but not Louis' life wasn't worth moving a little faster for?" She asked, slightly annoyed in that moment.

"Louis will be fine." J'ai stated, climbing into the carriage with Caroline right behind her.

"He was being tossed around like a toy last I saw! He could be dead!" She exclaimed and J'ai looked at her, and then began to laugh. "What is funny about this!?" She exclaimed.

"Caroline, you do know Louis is like me right?" J'ai asked, resting her hand on the ball of her hand. "He can't die, remember? The entirety of Primburogh is in far more danger than Louis will ever be." She trailed off when she saw the anger growing in the other girl's eyes.

"I don't care if he can pull the stars from the very sky! He's your friend, and someone most dear to me – the least you could do is show a little worry and concern even if he is in the same predicament as you. You take things far too lightly, and this is where the problem lies." She said, then quickly remembered who she was speaking to. "I'm…

sorry." She said softly, leaning back into the seat.

"I see." Was all that J'ai said for the remainder of the carriage ride, her eyes remaining fixated on the buildings passing by as they made their way back home.

While she was apologetic for the way she spoke to J'ai she was only expressing how she felt in the moment. J'ai showed little to no concern for anyone around her, least of all Louis or her own life. It almost made her wonder where she sat on the scale of concern in J'ai's mind. Did she even measure up as someone to concern herself with? She shook her head idly and turned her own gaze out the window, twirling her apron in her fingers nervously as they made their way through the streets. As they came into view of the manor her eyes widened as she saw black smoke billowing up from the roof of the large house. She gasped in a breath and locked eyes with the now burning building. J'ai sat in the carriage, staring at the same sight and let out a heavy sigh that was obviously annoyed, but then her gaze turned to Caroline.

"You will stay in the carriage, understood?" Her tone was stern.

"What about Louis?" She asked, tears daring to fall.

"You don't concern yourself with Louis right now, tell me that you understand my orders of staying inside the carriage. Do you understand?" She asked, and Caroline wanted to protest but caught sight of the darkness spreading around her.

Was this J'ai's anger? "Yes. I understand." She answered, unable to stand up to her Madam at this moment.

The carriage came to a stop, and without another word J'ai stepped out of the carriage. She handed the driver money and told him to stay before walking towards the manor. Wilhelm turned to see her walking towards the group of officers that was watching her home burn to the ground. She walked right past him as he began to speak to her about the boy, but he was taken aback by her cold demeanor as she walked right towards the flames. Other officers called out to her but all of their words fell on deaf ears. Wilhelm called them down, and simply watched her walk into the house as the flames licked around the upper floors. This was her home – had been ever since she was a child, and while she wouldn't admit it this place meant a lot to her.

Louis and the twisted officer stood in the upper hallway of the manor, both severely wounded as they looked towards one another. "Why won't you die?!" the Shadow within the officer exclaimed. "Surrender!" It added, lunging towards Louis again.

"Give up with the surrender shit!" Louis exclaimed, bracing for another charge.

There was a shrill shriek, and something warm and wet hit his hands and arms. He looked up and saw the officer impaled on the hidden blade of a cane sword, and lodged into the wall next to them. Louis stood straight and looked towards the stairs where J'ai stood with a look of burning rage.

"Madam!" He called out to her.

"Who started the fire?" J'ai exclaimed, looking to Louis who pointed at the officer struggling to release himself from the wall.

J'ai approached and the officer looked up to her with a sickly yellow gaze. "New vessel." It spoke in a gurgling voice, as the blade had run through its neck.

"Please, do come out of there. Makes things easier on both of us." She warned him, twisting the blade in his neck causing it to shriek in pain once more.

"Surrender!" It hissed back at her.

"You forget your position." She ripped the blade out of the wall and quickly shoved it up through its chin and out the top of its head. "You burned down my damn house! You have no right to order a surrender from me!" She hissed, watching that sickly yellow eye spiral out of control within the skull of the officer. "Now get out of there, because I doubt a dead host is of any use to a parasitic worm like you." A wild shriek erupted from within the officer as J'ai finished her words.

The shadow's tendril arm whipped around wildly, causing J'ai to back off. It gripped the blade in its chin and ripped it out. The officer's body went rigid and fell to the floor, beginning to seize frantically on the floor before a bulge appeared at the base of his neck then slowly traveled upward. Blood leaked from the man's mouth first, then a thick, yellow fleshy orb rolled out of his mouth. It opened to reveal an eye looking up to J'ai and Louis, before quickly slithering off down the hall. J'ai and Louis began to chase it, stopping only when it launched itself out the window and to the ground below.

An officer that heard the glass shatter looked up to see it falling. It landed on his face – he began to scream and roll around on the ground as everyone including Wilhelm watched as the eye forced its way into the man's mouth and down his throat. It was getting quicker with each body it jumped to, starting to understand the transition better with each time. It stood, the left eye of the man already that sickly yellow as it looked around at all the officers looking back at it.

"Shoot it!" J'ai yelled from the window. "Don't let it get away!" She added, and immediately Wilhelm gave the order to open fire.

None of the officers would have a chance as the shadow reached out with its tendril and grabbed the closest officer around the throat, throwing them into Wilhelm and the others in front of him. It then began to run at an incredible speed, carrying the shadow away and back towards the city. J'ai growled, and then her eyes widened as she looked back down to the Inspector and the officers.

"Wilhelm! Who's at the Prim with the boy and his father?" She asked.

"All hands on deck here, no one is there watching them!" He called back up to her, then his eyes widened. "Everyone! Back to the Prim, now!" He exclaimed, standing and pushing people off him.

"What is going on?" Louis asked as they made their way to the bottom of the burning manor. "What about the house?" He asked as they stepped outside.

"Let it burn, it's a relic of the past anyway. As for what's going on... that's harder to explain." She added, watching as all of Primburogh scrambled back to the station.

"Caroline?" He asked, and she looked back to him before nodding towards the last remaining carriage.

He started towards it but was stopped by an outstretched arm from J'ai. "You need to be more careful with her." She said, giving him a sideways glance. "You know what I mean. You're immortal, Louis – she is not. This could have ended far worse today." She said, finally lowering her arm. "Do better." She finished, turning back to watch what remained of her home burn to the ground. He just stared at her for a moment before nodding and rushing off to make sure Caroline was okay.

Chapter Fourteen

J'ai watched as the firemen rushed to kill the flames that ate away at her family home. Memories of her childhood – playing with young Wilhelm and Louis in the Prim. Watching her father work in the lab beneath the house, or her mother help cook in the kitchen. All of these memories, washed away in a single moment. Nothing but ash remained now, and a burning grew within her chest – her hand raised and came to rest over her heart. No tears – she did not deserve to cry, not for this.

"Madam..." She turned to see Louis and Caroline standing before her, both with a look of wonder, both looking to her for a solution.

"We should go to Primburogh. There is nothing more to be done here." Was all she would say on the matter, walking away towards the carriage that remained as she had told him. "Back to the Prim." She ordered, climbing halfway inside the carriage before looking back. Louis and Caroline now both stared at the still burning mansion. "Let's go!" She ordered. "There is no point in staring. We have a job to finish!" Both turned back to her.

Caroline was in tears as she stepped into the carriage, Louis doing his best to stay strong in the moment just as J'ai had chosen to do, but the anger burned inside her – growing like a cancer deep within her. Louis dared a glance to her, and saw his mistress sitting with her arms crossed and eyes closed – clearly deep in thought. He was worried though, worried about what would happen. Of course J'ai likely had the funds to find a new home, but that wasn't the point. That was their last connection to who they were before... this. All that time and research, lost in an instant.

"Damn it!" J'ai hissed, giving the carriage door a kick. "Damn it – damn it!" She exhaled a breath then, and ran a hand through her hair. "We'll find that… *thing*, and destroy it. I swear on all that is left of me, it will regret the day it crossed me." She grumbled angrily as she glared at Louis.

He nodded in confirmation. "Any of us. The manor was all of our homes – we have all lost today." He put a hand on Caroline's arm.

"You and I lost more than you realize… I was so close, I think." She said, leaning back and tilting her head back. "So close…"

The carriage arrived at the Prim, and it seemed all the patrolmen were on high alert. Four standing out front, watching the carriage closely as it came to a stop in front of them. J'ai opened the door and looked down at the guns pointed up at her, and scoffed before walking passed them. Louis and Caroline were right behind her, Caroline holding fast to Louis' arm as she looked at the guns and then forward to a confident J'ai pushing past the front doors of the building.

"Where's Wilhelm?" She called out, and turned her attention to where the first officer pointed, seeing the man standing near the front desk. "I need to see that boy, now." She said, and Wilhelm turned towards her.

"He's clammed up, just like his father." He said, shrugging lightly. "I don't think you're going to get through to him like you did his old man." Wilhelm added and J'ai narrowed her gaze.

"Kids love me." She said coldly as she walked past him. "What room?" She asked, glancing back.

"First on the left, two doors before his father's." He said, shaking his head before looking back towards Louis and Caroline. "Oh… wait – you two?" He asked, pointing between them.

"Yes." Louis answered swiftly. "What happened around here?" He asked, still confused about everything going on.

"Beats me – hard to follow honestly. Something about a door, and now this *thing*." He sighed and shook his head.

J'ai opened the door, the chair clattering to the floor as the boy pressed himself into the corner of the room just as his father had before. It was good to see there were no lasting effects from the being taking the body hostage, she was sure the poor patrolman at her home was not as lucky however. She was lucky she even guessed correctly that a host near death was of no use to the creature. She approached him and knelt down to his level, placing a hand on his back and gently rubbing in a circular motion – almost soothing in a way. She felt his tensity and trembling slowly lessen and she hummed thoughtfully.

"My mother used to do this for me when I was upset, always worked like magic." She said, and the boy slowly turned his head to look at her. "There you are, Jack isn't it?" She asked and he nodded slowly. "Tell me what happened. I need to know so we can stop the monster." His eyes widened and he turned, gripping her arms desperately.

"Don't look." He muttered. "Don't look at it. Don't look at it." He said over and over, as though they were the only words he could muster.

She eyed him for a moment, and sighed softly. "What is it?" She asked, and his eyes became distant.

"Shadow." He whispered before he began to shake again.

"Okay, Jack. That will be enough." She stood, but he would cling to her. "Don't worry, I'll fetch your father." Tears came to his eyes.

"Dad?" He asked, and she nodded. "Dad!" he exclaimed, releasing her – backing into the corner with a mixture of fear and excitement that was clearly overwhelming him.

She exited the room – Wilhelm, Louis, and Caroline were there waiting for her. "What was that?" Wilhelm asked, and she shrugged.

"Good news is that I think he might recover from this trauma. He's young, and right now he will be scared but I think he'll cover this memory. Bad news is that I don't have much to go on about this *Shadow* other than not to look at it." She rubbed her chin thoughtfully, then snapped her fingers. "Right, fetch the boy's father. They can go together again." She said, waving her hand passively.

"Finally." Wilhelm muttered and motioned for an officer to approach, then ordered him to put the man with his son. "Well what happens now? This thing is running around the city, we can't just sit around." He said, ruffling his own hair in aggravation.

"There isn't much of an option, it's likely changed skins again, and who knows who it could be about now." She shook her head. "I hate it as much as you do." She added, crossing her own arms.

"What about you?" Wilhelm asked, turning his eyes to J'ai.

"What about me?" She retorted, stepping out of the way as Peter was guided into the room to reunite with his son. "If you're asking about the manor, don't. I'll simply have to go elsewhere for living arrangements." She said, shrugging.

"What about Louis and Caroline?" He asked, turning his eyes to them.

"I follow the Madam wherever she goes." Louis stated confidently.

"Me too." Caroline added with a nod.

"I have money saved in case such an incident were to occur, though it was more on the chance of a lab incident rather than an entity from some unknown world." She said, looking to Wilhelm. "For now an apartment in the city will do. It will be loud, but it will do." J'ai said, looking at Louis, who nodded softly.

"I'll begin looking for a free space." He said, bowing slightly.

"Now hold on." Wilhelm stated. "I live in a pretty decent building – not as shabby as you'd expect, J'ai." He stated, coldly as he turned his gaze to her.

"I've said no such thing." She chided, turning her gaze from him.

"Not true, but we'll come back to that. Either way there are two rooms available in the building. Fairly big and one has enough space for an office." He said, shrugging slightly as he described the place.

"Sounds like you were interested." J'ai pointed out as she eyed him for a moment.

"I was… but you lot seem to be hard up at the moment. The rooms would be better suited to you three. 'Sides I was just throwing the option out there to save Louis some leg work." He added, waving his own hand passively.

J'ai nodded, then looked to Louis who returned her gaze.

For a moment there was silence and then both nodded a final time. They started to walk away from the Inspector, who turned and watched them go with confusion. Did this mean yes? Were they not even going to acknowledge the idea? He shook his head and sighed heavily, rubbing the back of his neck before turning down the hall and looking through the one-way window. Peter and his son sat crying, hugging one another as Peter would lean back and hold his son's face in his hands. This was the one good thing to come from this strange day – at least a family was brought back together. It was a bittersweet ending though as they lost the Shadow, and he lost two officers.

"What the hell is going on in this city?" He asked himself, crossing his arms as he just stood there watching the two in the other room.

It sat atop a building that overlooked Primburogh, its sickly eye watching as the trio walked out and boarded another carriage. It followed the carriage with its eye until it faded from view, then turned back to the Prim. Memories from the vessel it harbored now told everything the Shadow needed to know. He stood straight, raising and flexing its hand, and then relaxing it before allowing his arm to fall back to his side. These bodies were weak, the older the body the less time the Shadow seemed to have within it. The boy was the best vessel – a child, yes.

"I must find a new host." He said, the Shadow's understanding of this language seemingly growing.

It was clear to the Shadow that a mortal vessel would never last as long as he would like – the perfect vessels escaped him for now. It was clear from the strength of the male, and the fearlessness within the female. The hair stood on the back of his vessel's neck, and his eyes narrowed. He delved into the memories of the patrolman, and smirked. J'ai – a name was known. A monster – yes, that was a word the Shadow understood, a universal name for his kind by many who have been trapped within their realm.

"The woman's male slave must be mine." He spoke to himself as he came to a stop above an alley, dropping down out of sight before stepping out into the street. "For now, I must rest." His eyes locked with a young boy walking with his mother. "It will do." He walked towards the pair.

The woman looked away from the boy for a mere moment, and like a carnivore took the opportunity to scoop up the boy. The boy screamed and the woman screamed after him, calling the name of her son as she watched him being carried off. A pair of street officers gave chase, blowing their whistles as they watched the male figure duck down an alley. They would cut the corner and see the man lying face down on the ground, the legs of the boy trembling as they poked from behind some trash. One officer rushed to the boy, lifting him up as his eyes opened slowly and looked up to the copper. The other officer approached the man lying face down on the ground.

He flipped the man over, and saw the familiar pants of the Primburogh uniform, foam dripping from his lips as his hands clenched over his chest. He was dead. "What the bloody hell?" The officer questioned, scratching beneath his cap.

"I'll get the lad back to his mother – it seems it was his lucky day." He said ,standing with the boy in his arms. "Don't look son, you shouldn't see such a thing." The officer stated, patting the boy's back.

"Mummy…?" The boy muttered as he stared at the corpse as they walked away.

"No worries son, she's right here." He said, waving towards the frightened woman.

"Thomas!" She called, rushing towards them.

Chapter Fifteen

The manor's burning did cause some setbacks – momentary ones, but setbacks nonetheless. Because of this, J'ai, Louis, and of course young Caroline had to find new living arrangements for a temporary time. The building Wilhelm stayed in was, as he said, not as shabby as she'd initially expected. The room he spoke about was bigger than he described, a rather spacious loft and of course there was another room on the same floor that was for rent that J'ai quickly scooped up for Louis and Caroline. No time was wasted in making these new spaces their own, and somehow Wilhelm and his wife had been taken on as new employees to J'ai – somehow.

It started with one kind gesture, some homemade biscuits and warm tea to welcome their new neighbors and friends, next thing he knows his wife comes back down with a uniform similar to Caroline's and she's expressing excitement over a job. He would admit that J'ai was oddly nicer to him now, even more so to his wife. Perhaps only because she hired her temporarily to help Caroline clean the rooms out and redecorate.

"You can't just tear up the carpeting!" He turned to the familiar voice of the building owner. "Ms. Mauvais please, you do not own this building, you can't simply start tearing apart my floors and walls at your leisure!" He bellowed desperately as he followed behind her.

"This man." She muttered as she stopped before Louis, handing him his post.

"Did you go through my letterbox again?" He asked, both ignoring the landlord's words now.

"I did. You never have anything entertaining to look at." She huffed, tossing her own letters into his hand as well. "Burn them, it seems my mail is as entertaining as yours." She added and finally turned toward the landlord.

"Mr. Gallons." She began reaching into her pants pocket and pulling forth a few notes.

"It's Tallows…" He corrected her.

"I don't care." She replied quickly, holding the money out to him. "I rented the rooms, yes? Here is double what you charge for those rooms, and I will continue to pay you this much if you simply go away. Your carpets are blue, your walls are blue. The bloody hallway is blue!" She exhaled a sharp breath. "You're lucky I don't burn the building to the ground. Now, if you want to continue to line your chubby little pockets with my money then be a darling and disappear… if not I'll make you disappear like–"

"J'ai!" Wilhelm hissed from behind.

"It's just that blue was my mother's favorite color, and that's what she wanted the rooms to look like. So I don't think I'm willing to just let you change all that just because you hand me some extra rent, mum." Mr. Tallows stated, trying to hand the money back.

Wilhelm just shook his head from behind her. "No." Was all J'ai said, glaring at him. "You will take it." She stated, clearly getting annoyed with this man. She was not used to people refusing her like this.

"I will not, now I insist you stop these renovations or you can find somewhere else to live." His tone had become sharper, and J'ai's eyes narrowed.

"Louis!" She called out in a calm, almost too casual tone.

"J'ai no!" Wilhelm hissed, pulling her back into his

apartment motioning for the landlord to wait just a moment. "You can't do this, you cannot strong-arm and bully your way through everything." He stated, pointing at her. "This is how things work in these types of buildings." He said, clearly begging her at this point. "Please – for the love of my family and all that is holy – do not kill my landlord." At that statement she cocked her head in clear confusion.

"Wilhelm, I wasn't going to kill the man." She said with an airy laugh.

"Madam, you called for me?" Louis stepped into the room, staring at J'ai as she looked over her shoulder at him.

"Nothing Lou-Lou, never mind." She said, waving her hand passively.

"You were!" He said in a whispered hiss as he jabbed an accusatory finger at her.

"He is insufferable – you know I hate blue!" She hissed back at him.

"What is wrong with you? Who comes to the conclusion that murder is the answer?" He asked, genuine confusion in his voice.

"The kind of person who doesn't have to worry about sitting in prison for a few years over a landlord murder." She added, crossing her arms. "Anything less than twenty years is no more than a blink." She added.

He shook his head at her. "No." Was all he said, almost like talking to a toddler. "You will not kill the landlord! Say it." He ordered, and for a moment they simply glared at one another until finally she sighed.

"Fine." Was all she was going to say.

"Say it..." His tone was serious, and it forced another sigh from within her.

"I will not kill the landlord." She grumbled. "However I'm still changing the carpets and walls. He will not stop me." She stated and turned away from him as she began to walk away.

"For an immortal you're quite the child." Wilhelm chided, following her to the door.

She merely grumbled a response, glaring at the landlord as she pouted her way past him and up the stairs towards the sounds of renovations. Mr. Tallows shook his head, he was a chubby man with a well shaved head and face. He dressed like a man that worked the docks, something he likely carried over from his past. A soft spoken man for the most part, it came to a surprise to Wilhelm when the man had hollered earlier, or at least raised his voice ever so slightly. Then again, J'ai hadn't been her ordinary self either – for the most part she was calm and collected as usual, but recently she's grown a specific fondness for him and his wife – meaning she wasn't nearly as rude or mean to him as she normally would be.

"That woman, Wilhelm." Mr. Tallows stated before taking in a long breath of air. "My mum always told me 'Leonel, don't be hittin' ladies now.' Oh Lord help me, because that one up there tests me on the daily." He said, shaking his head.

Wilhelm chuckled. "Don't let Louis hear you say that." He said, turning back to his room.

"I'd blow him over with a puff of air – have you seen the lad?" He asked with a hearty laugh that Wilhelm awkwardly shared.

"I have…" He nodded slowly with a knowing smile. "I have seen him. Boy might not look like much but trust me, you'd not leave a mark on him and you'd look like the baker's twisted rolls."

Mr. Tallows followed him into his apartment. "How's the missus?" He asked, shoving his hands into his pockets.

"Oh, she's alright. Had a bit of an issue this morning but nothing major. Got a little sick is all, J'ai surprisingly enough was very helpful. Gave her some medicine to soothe her stomach." He said with a smile.

"Ah, so that's where the lady gets her money and help. Wasn't aware women could be doctors – times are changing they are." He said, rubbing his chin. "Better for it I suppose – women have better bedside manners I'm sure, not to mention better with the little ones." He added with a laugh.

Wilhelm shrugged – he genuinely had no opinion on the matter. It'd been almost three months since the Shadow case – the Queen's finely dressed lap dog swooped in and was sure to inform everyone at the Prim that what they'd seen was to be reported on as nothing more than a crazed police officer that had a sick mind and a drive to kidnap boys. It still pissed him off, using his own officers as cover for some weird happenings. People died – two officers died, and a few more injured from that day, and then there was Jack and Peter… they had disappeared too. J'ai said they were likely carted off to some asylum where they'd never be able to talk about it, a place where no one would ever believe them. That thing was still out there – he was sure of it, and he knew J'ai was sure of it too.

There was a soft knock at his door-frame – both men turned to see young Caroline standing in the doorway, and then she would bow slightly. "Inspector Goddard, not to panic

150

you sir but J'ai sent me to tell you your wife has fainted upstairs." Wilhelm was pushing past her the moment the word fainted left Caroline's lips.

"Izzy!" He called out, almost falling at the top of the steps as he pushed into the room.

J'ai sat on the edge of the couch, listening to his wife's heart through a stethoscope, taking it off as he dropped to his knees next to her. Caroline returned not long after, Mr. Tallows behind her. Despite J'ai's visible dislike for him being here, she knew there wasn't much she could say about it at the moment. Wilhelm spoke softly to the woman he called Izzy – Elizabeth Kinsley – a young women he'd met by chance as she passed by a crime scene. Romantic – of that J'ai was sure.

"Don't worry, she's fine. Exhausted, and needs to be taking better care of herself for the next… oh…" She hummed thoughtfully and shrugged to Louis on the opposite side of the room. "Seven to eight months, give or take." J'ai finished tucking the stethoscope into her pocket.

"What? why?" Wilhelm was starting to panic. "Is she sick?" He was desperate for a clear answer.

"No, you idiot. She's pregnant." J'ai scoffed and shook her head. "She must have known, and clearly didn't want to tell you." She sat down in a chair across from the sofa. "A secret lover perhaps?" She gave a fake gasp to hide the coy smirk on her face. "Wilhelm, father to a bastard child." She chuckled.

"Shut up – that's ugly even from you." He hissed, but she merely chuckled at his outburst.

"Either way, you should take better care of her for the time being. You two have some things to talk about." She watched him begin to dote on her already, taking a dampened cloth from Caroline and placing it on her forehead. "Congratulations, by the way." She added, and immediately the mood changed.

"Aye, this calls for a toast. I'll go and grab me finest bottle of rum." Mr. Tallows stated, turning back out the door.

"I kind of hope we're still here when the baby is born... I love babies." Caroline stated, and Louis visibly lost color to his complexion.

"Babies are loud and smell horrible." J'ai stated, but then shrugged. "I suppose that's just what babies do though, other than that they are alright." She would glance at Louis. "What about you, Louis?" She smirked, clearly bored and taking any opportunity to mess with someone. "What do you think of babies?" She asked, and immediately he cleared his throat and shrugged.

"As you said. They are... alright." He wouldn't look to Caroline – he was afraid to see if she was disappointed or even looking at him at all. "Congratulations, Wilhelm." He would add, trying to divert the conversation away from him.

"Pregnant... I... I haven't the first clue about being a father." He said, slumping back onto the floor as the reality finally hit him.

"No one has any idea about parenting their first go of it." J'ai stated, taking a cigarette from the case and lighting it. "I've seen you though, Willy. Seen how you treat those street kids that hang around the alley by the Prim, saw how well you handled that boy, Jack. You'll be a... sufficient father." She said, exhaling smoke from her lungs just as the landlord came back with the rum.

"Oi!" He exclaimed, pointing to J'ai. "No smoking in here!

Take that outside if you're going to be smoking around here." He ordered and J'ai growled.

"Damn. Was sort of hoping you'd have tripped going down the stairs." She said, putting the cigarette out on the back of the cigarette case. "Caroline, were there any other letters delivered here today?" She asked, slumping in her chair as the landlord started passing around filled cups.

"No Madam, if you're waiting for word from the Queen I've not seen any of those strange letters or that man." She said, shaking her head softly.

J'ai groaned, and took a long drink of the rum when her cup finally got to her. "I'm so bored." She mumbled.

"I think I will take Lizzy back to our room, she needs to rest now. Thank you, J'ai." He said, gently lifting her and making his way out of the room.

"Louis, make sure he doesn't drop the poor woman down the steps." She said and Louis nodded and turned to follow Wilhelm.

She watched for a moment as they filed out, Mr. Tallows babbling on as he too walked behind the men. She was left alone with Caroline then, and her own thoughts on the matter. Oddly enough, she didn't have any real negative thoughts or feelings about this matter. Kids were one of the few things J'ai didn't really view negatively – aside from the behavior issues some may have but to her that was at the fault of the parent and a lack of discipline. Then again she would never know the hardships of parenthood, she refused to get involved in such affairs. For now though she would stay around, finish renovating this hell-scape and finally get all her affairs in order so that she could begin the reconstruction of the manor, but during all of that investigating the Shadow. The Prim may have given up but she wouldn't, she was not about to entertain the thought of allowing such a thing to continue living in this world without consequence.

Chapter Sixteen

Wailing – endless wailing. This is all that infants did – day in and day out, crying their little lungs out – it was maddening. All the time of Elizabeth's pregnancy there hadn't been a single letter from the Queen's little servant, and in all that time Wilhelm and his wife had become almost like family within her own little circle. Louis seemed to keep a close eye on Elizabeth, even before J'ai had officially told him to, and Caroline was always there to help whenever she needed it – which was greatly appreciated by Wilhelm to say the least.

As the seasons changed, however, it became more and more difficult for doctors to come to the house. Illness filled the hospitals making going impossible, and that left it up to J'ai when the time of the birth finally came around. She was prepared for a normal birth – she was not prepared for a premature labor however, and neither was anyone else. Louis and Wilhelm were removed from the room – the memory was still fresh – the struggle, and the blood. She hadn't felt such stress in so many years – she couldn't even remember the last time she felt such desperation, but the wailing – she'd not expected the wailing. The child that fell into her hands cried so desperately for a mother that would never reach out to hold them.

Looking down at the little girl crying in her hands, the blood on her sleeves – it was the first time in many years since her own family passed away that she felt this strange slowing of time. Aware of every breath she took – the amplified wails of the little one, and then finally the pull back to reality as Caroline carefully took the child from her – wrapping her in a soft towel. It was like a dream as she watched Caroline take the child to be washed off quickly, while J'ai gently pulled the sheet over Elizabeth's blank, pale face. She took in a breath and made her way to the door, and opened it up to see Wilhelm sitting in the hall, staring up at her desperately as the door closed behind her.

Wailing – endless wailing.

Her eyes opened to the sound of the infant crying – the sound alone raising a dagger within her chest. "Caroline!" She called out, the woman quickly appearing in the doorway of her apartment. "That child needs feeding." She said, pointing back out towards the hall from her seat.

"I know, ma'am… but Mr. Goddard won't allow anyone in the apartment… won't allow anyone near little Hailey." She said, a clear look of desperation of her own.

J'ai growled and tossed her mail into the fireplace in front of her. "Enough of this. Louis!" She called out.

"Yes, Madam?" Louis questioned, stepping out of his and Caroline's room.

"Door. Open it. Now." She ordered, pointing to Wilhelm's apartment.

With a shrug Louis started walking down the stairs, Caroline protested stating it might not be the best idea – Wilhelm was still mourning. None of it was listened to, for Louis did as he was told despite his lover's pleading and easily kicked the door in. The sound of the child's crying exploded in full force into the building's hall. J'ai entered, Caroline close behind as she went for the pram, and Hailey. J'ai motioned towards Wilhelm's room, and Louis nodded as he made his way to gather the man himself up.

"I'll have Louis take the pram up to my room for now." J'ai stated, crossing her arms.

"Ma'am?" Caroline questioned as she bounced the infant in her arms to quieten her.

"Just go tend to the girl, I'll handle this." Was all she said as she made her own way to Wilhelm's room.

"Piss off!" She heard Wilhelm's voice crack angrily as she stepped into the darkened room. "The lot of ya, git outta my house!" He bellowed drunkenly.

"That's enough, Wilhelm." J'ai stated coldly.

"No! It'll never be enough! Get out!" He hollered, throwing a bottle at the wall near her head.

"I plan on it. Hailey goes with me though until you've cleaned your act up. You're a man, Wilhelm, and yet here you are having a fit like a child." She scoffed, shaking her head as she approached him. "I understand you fault me, but I'll tell you that it would have ended the same no matter what." She stated, seeing the fire spark in his eyes then.

"You don't know that! A real doctor might have saved her rather than mutilated her like you did!" He yelled, jabbing a finger at J'ai then – Louis stepping in only to keep Wilhelm from going any farther. "I'll die before I let Hailey stay even a moment alone with you! *Monster*!" He hissed from behind Louis.

"No, had it been a real doctor the chances of both your wife and child being dead would have been the likelier outcome. I had to make a choice, the child or Elizabeth…" She trailed off – going back in her mind for a moment it seems. "I chose the child." She turned her back to him then. "When you're done thinking of yourself and your own pain, Hailey will be with myself and Caroline." She would glance back at him briefly. "Waiting for her father." She added, leaving the moment at that.

"Bitch-!" Wilhelm hissed, but was knocked backward by a

swift crack to the mouth from the back of Louis' hand.

"Madam might be cold, cruel even, but you neglect to realize she had only the best interest at heart. You weren't in the room-"

"Neither were you!" Wilhelm interrupted, wiping a small drip of blood from his lip. "Neither of us were in that damn room!" He exclaimed, tears forming to his eyes. "I should have been in there…" He sobbed.

"No, I wasn't in the room, but Caroline was… she told me everything. I promised not to say anything to you, but if it will get you off your ass and back to work and caring for *your* daughter then talk to Caroline – get what you can out of her, and understand what she and J'ai both went through." She exhaled a soft breath and moved to the door. "Like everyone else you're so quick to assume J'ai had only malice intentions in her actions that night, but never stop to think about what toll it might have taken on her to make such a choice." He would watch Wilhelm turn his back to him staring out his bedroom window. "Get well Wilhelm." Louis finished closing the door behind him.

Silence. The crying stopped, he was left alone with nothing more than the silent mumbling of his own mind. Tears trailed down his cheeks, the memory of that same silence that filled his soul when J'ai stepped out of the room. Before the door slowly closed shut behind her he saw the still feet beneath the bloodied sheet on the table in the center of their living area. He knew before the words even left J'ai's lips, but the moment they did he remembered the crumble that came over him. All will in his body left him, and he collapsed like a child in front of J'ai, and Louis. Wailing, his cries mixing in with that of his own daughter's.

Wailing – endless wailing.

158

Time moves on though, and with time life gets easier. J'ai paid forward the money needed to rebuild her family home, Louis proposed to Caroline, life continued to move for them. Faster to J'ai than most others, but she still found the time to relax, and think about what life has brought for her in almost a year's time already. She wondered why no letters had been coming, no new orders. She was surprised how silent the Shadow had been, even wondered if maybe that one would rear its ugly head again – she was sure with enough time it would. Patience was key – patience was something she had to learn.

Wilhelm made no effort towards being a father – no effort to return to Primburogh. He was trapped it seemed, in a timeless place where the only thing that console him was the memory of his Elizabeth and the drink. The baby was happy though, little Hailey Goddard – an absolute angel, as Caroline calls her. She and Louis had taken the brunt of parental responsibility with the child while J'ai did her best not to get attached. She would admit though that even she had developed a small soft spot for the infant, despite the numerous annoyances that come with raising a child.

"Louis." She spoke from her seat as she looked over the day's news. "It seems they've put on a new Inspector." J'ai stated, holding the paper up to Louis as he fed the baby.

"Unfortunate. I suppose that puts truth to our suspicions that Wilhelm will not be returning to work." He would sigh softly, shaking his head.

"We should visit him." J'ai stated, folding the paper over the arm of her chair.

"He keeps the doors locked, I can't keep kicking his door down or the landlord will remove us." Louis stated as he began to burp the child. "Hailey will be a year old… he's not held her since that night… not even looked at her." He glanced down at the child.

There was a long moment of silence from J'ai as she stared at the back of the infant now nodding off on Louis' shoulder. "She will grow up to look like her mother." She said suddenly. "He's afraid of her because he cannot let Elizabeth go." She turned her gaze away and stared into the fireplace. "If I can already see it, then surely he didn't miss it." She added, closing her eyes as she allowed her head to rest on her hand.

"I'm surprised that you've allowed him to go this long." Louis said, pulling her gaze back to him. "You talk about him like Elizabeth's death only changed him. It's clear Madam, and forgive me for being out of line, but it has changed you as well." He noted how she simply looked away from him once more. "You… feel sorry for him, and guilty because of what you had to do… There is no shame in that. You allow him to wallow in his pain while you dwell on the possibility that his suffering was your doing." He shook his head then. "You did your best."

"Enough!" She yelled – the child startled in Louis' arms began to cry. "You have no idea what I think, or what I feel – you're a butler, not my therapist! Get out!" She waved her hand aggressively, and Louis sighed.

"Here then." He said, approaching her and placing the now crying baby in her lap.

"What the- Louis?" She questioned, watching him walk away.

"If you want to blame yourself, and allow Wilhelm to continue on the path that he is… then take responsibility." He said motioning to the child. "I'm your butler, not a babysitter." He added, and closed the door behind him.

J'ai stared at the door for a moment then felt the sudden movement of the child in her lap as Hailey slowly tilted backwards as she cried. Quickly J'ai put her hands on the child's sides to keep her from falling. She has held Hailey before, but never have they been left alone together. The child continued to cry, and slowly J'ai lifted the infant to her shoulder and bounced her but the wailing never ended – not for her. Flashes of blood – the wailing – the way Elizabeth looked at her right before J'ai had to cut her open. The wailing. Without her realizing, tears began to trickle down her cheeks – she couldn't stop them.

"It's okay…" She said softly to the child in her arms. "I'm sorry…" She whispered as her own tears began to flow stronger. "I'm so sorry." Her voice cracked.

Please forgive me.

Chapter Seventeen

Time moves quickly – more quickly than some of us care to realize. Before we know it, time has gotten away from us, and we forget what was supposed to be most important. Age reminds us of the things we've forgotten, reminds us of the people we left behind. It is said that time heals all wounds as well – how long it takes is never disclosed – we just know that over time the wounds caused by time slowly heal. We often forget what hurt us, other times we simply move away from that painful place… working our way back onto the path we should have never left in the first place.

A knock came to J'ai's flat door – she opened it and Mr. Cordel stood before her. "Good afternoon ,Madam." Simon stated, stepping in past her slightly, his eyes looking around the flat as it was his first time in this room. "Not what I would have expected from someone such as you, but I suppose it works." He said, clasping his hands in front of him as to avoid touching anything.

"Simon. it's been some time." J'ai stated, crossing her arms as she watched the man before her. "What do you want?" J'ai asked with a cold tone.

"The usual. The Queen has a job for you." He stated, holding a letter out to her. "It's the Shadow." He said, J'ai's gaze turning to him immediately.

She stood and walked over to him, snatching the letter from his hands and looking at the sealed envelope. "She had people investigating it all this time? I've not heard a single word." She didn't look at Simon as she stared at the envelope.

"All efforts were focused on the Shadow. At present the entity was more important than anything else. Besides, it gives you a chance to finish this job, since you failed the first time." He said, a coy smirk pulling over his lips.

"Fine. This time keep Primburogh out of it. The less they know the better." She said turning back to him. "That will be all, you may leave." She said, motioning for him to leave then.

"Not going to read it?" He asked, stepping back towards the door.

"On my own time." She stated, walking back to her chair and tossing it down on the arm.

"I've heard Wilhelm quit his position at Primburogh. Was it because of the Shadow incident?" Simon asked, staying by the door.

"Wilhelm…" She whispered his name – silently she would look back to the man over her shoulder. "He had some issues of his own... he is still dealing with them." She said, leaving it at that.

"As long as he knows he can never utter a word of what he's seen, I care little of what he's going through." Simon replied coldly.

"You don't have to worry about that" Simon turned to the voice behind him, J'ai leaned forward to get a look as well from her place near her chair. "I could care less about what goes on out there any more." Wilhelm's voice was tired, hair peppered gray and disheveled from such a long time without being cut. Mixed with the stubble growing on his face, he resembled a man J'ai had never met before.

"I see. It's a shame you feel that way about your country now." Simon stepped past him, and gave a nod of farewell to J'ai, leaving her and Wilhelm to stare at one another for a long moment before finally motioning him into her flat.

Time changes everyone. Ten years was a long time for a normal person, but for J'ai she found it was a passing moment, something easily missed. Louis was learning too with each passing day as Caroline grew older without him. Married, and yet to have children of their own – they came to take baby Hailey in as their own especially without Wilhelm showing any interest in her. Until recently, that is. With time Wilhelm eventually saw what he was doing, not only to his daughter but to himself. He was living in the shadows of ghosts, living each day in a bright world of memories where he didn't have to leave Elizabeth behind. Back in a time where nothing mattered but each other.

"Ten years! You locked yourself away for ten goddamn years, Wilhelm!" Louis exclaimed, J'ai sat quietly in her chair as she read through the day's mail – it had become routine.

"I know… I couldn't…" Wilhelm couldn't seem to find the words to explain himself.

"Your daughter needed you!" Louis continued.

Wilhelm balled his hands into fists. "I know!" He exclaimed, directing his gaze up to Louis. "You think I don't know? I messed up, I know. I missed so much – my little girl has grown up and she doesn't even know who I am." He lowered his gaze. "I owe you so much... all of you." His words were soft. "I don't expect to just have her handed over to me, you and Caroline… and J'ai – she only knows you three." He chuckled and shook his head, tears forming in his eyes. "I just… want a single chance to see her." He looked to J'ai, her eyes staring back as the words left him.

"She knows about you." J'ai stated matter-of-factually, Wilhelm's eyes looked to her in shock. "Louis… tell him." She said, turning her eyes back to the letter in her hand.

"Caroline and I are not so cruel to completely erase you from her life." He said looking down at the disheveled man before him with sympathy in his gaze. "It does, however, make me happy to know you… aren't here to take her." He said and Wilhelm chuckled as the tears rolled down his cheeks. "She knows that Caroline and I are not her parents, we simply raised her. She does call us as her parents, but she knows who her father is, what his name is." Wilhelm choked back more tears and then fell to the floor on his knees.

"Thank you…" He whispered, wrapping his arms around Louis' left leg as he sobbed. "Thank you, Louis." He repeated, unable to hold back the tears any longer. "Thank you so much, I can never repay this debt to you." He wept at Louis' feet.

Time means everything. Despite their predicament, they understood the value of time, and of life. Most people never know how much time they have left in the world, mortals sometimes take their time for granted and by the time they pick themselves up it's too late. The Shadow, it seemed, took advantage of this. Using time as a method to hide itself from the world, ten years was a long time, and only now things were starting to come out? J'ai was skeptical – the letter in hand described the same madness she saw in Peter when she first spoke to him – the fear and desperation in him, but what she was reading was far more extreme. Fear so strong the mind was left completely broken, victims left in endless terror, constantly screaming for someone to save them.

"Louis… It's time to pick Haliey up from school." She looked to Wilhelm, then back down to the letter in her hands. "I think today would be a good time for you two to have your reunion." She said, closing the letter and tossing it aside with the rest of her mail.

"Are you sure, Madam?" Louis asked, finding her focus on this moment strangely unlike her. "Is there time for it?" He added to the question, and J'ai's eyes locked to his.

"We'll make time." She said, crossing her arms and turning her eyes back to the fire.

Ten years is a long time to think about what has brought us to this point; a long time for J'ai to think about how she ended up where she was in her life, how she came to be how she was as a person. Ten years of finally asking herself what the hell she was thinking back then, why she would think what she was doing was at all right. Ten years of coming to terms with the fact that she had been no different than the shadow back then, using people and corpses to a means of an end, ultimately for selfish reasons for no one other than herself. She began her journey seeking a way to bring back someone she loved more than even herself, her dearest little brother. In her journey she ended up costing herself, and her dear friend Louis the right to die. She stole it from him, albeit accidentally, but either way she stole his life from him.

It takes time to come to terms with these facts – she could see Louis was slowly becoming more anxious with each passing day – each passing year that Caroline ages without him. Now, with time, Wilhelm had come to his senses, wanting to make up for time he'd lost with his daughter because of his own obsession with the past. J'ai could relate, she'd spent a long time obsessing over her own mistake, and how she could get back on track. Now, she accepts that her brother is dead – he will never come back. Dead is dead, but she couldn't turn back the clock now it was too late for regret. Now she had to figure out what to tell Louis – how could she tell him that with the fire all her research she had on possibly curing them was lost… how does she tell him she has to start over?

"J'ai…" She turned her eyes to Louis as they rode to the pick-up spot for Hailey. She didn't remember getting into the carriage, her mind making her lose time as she pulled herself deep in thought. "You seem distracted these days. Is everything alright Madam?" Louis asked, genuine concern in his voice.

"Louis… are you really my friend?" She asked, leaning back and turning her eyes out the window of the carriage.

"Of course. We've been together since we were children. I made a promise." He answered, tilting his head as he watched her.

"No, forget the contract. Are you my *friend*, Louis? Do you care about me beyond some stupid piece of paper my father made yours sign?" She asked, her gaze turning back to him with an emotion he'd never seen in her before.

Desperation?
Loneliness?
Worry…?

"… Of course. J'ai, you're the only friend I've known despite how our families became tied together." He said, watching as her gaze slowly turned away from him once again. "Are you… alright?" He asked again, this time his tone was far more gentle.

There was a long moment of silence between them until the school finally came into view. "I'm not sure Louis… for once I genuinely do not know if I am alright." She answered, taking in a long breath.

The Shadow had plenty of time as well, growing up in a human body it had taken time to get used to how things worked, and how one was meant to behave if they were to go unnoticed. School was a good way to blend in, though the majority of human students longed for the end of school days, the Shadow found the time within these institutions far beyond educational in the perception of a human child. It learned a lot about this world's history, and this world's concept of time. Most of all, the Shadow learned of a certain someone that carried the scent of his enemies all over her. She reeked of that man and woman who stood up to him in his raw form – the woman that looked into his eyes without fear.

He learned her name was Hailey; the woman that brought her to school most of the time was who he recognized first, barely remembering her other than the sweet taste of her fear as she ran from the manor that fateful day. Caroline is the name he remembered the butler calling her by. His vessel was older than the young girl before the maid – she was likely only ten, maybe eleven he couldn't tell just by looking. Ever since that day he spent most of his free time watching the girl, stalking her and learning all he could about not just her but the people in her life that seemingly took care of her. So his enemy did have a weakness after all? It made him drool with excitement – even now as he watched J'ai and Louis themselves arrive at the school. He wanted to do it now, swoop down and lob the child's head off right in front of them, laughing as they crumbled in front of him. He wanted it so much – to break that woman who lived without fear – who dared to look at him with those very eyes devoid of what sustains him.

This time he would look back into those eyes, and this time she would have fear in them. He would be sure of that.

Chapter Eighteen

Stumbling feet carry the young woman down the foggy alleyway, her make-up smudged, and a drunken smile painted her features as she continued forward. What she couldn't have known, or been aware of were the eyes that watched her. As she walked the sound of heavier steps filtered in from behind her – slowly she stopped and turned only to see no one was there. There is a kind of fear that fills a person when they become aware of their surroundings – of their own vulnerability. It cleaves us near in two, but that fear is something magnificent, and powerful if harnessed.

She turned, a gasp escaping her as she bumped into the chest of someone taller than her. Her glossy gaze lifted, the face of the one in front of her was obscured by the shadow cast from the brim of his black hat. Her lips parted, but his hand was over her mouth in an instant – the sound of her struggling filled the alley, the wet sound of metal piercing flesh, a pool of blood that filtered to the center of the walkway and dripped down into the gutter. He straddled her corpse, near sitting on her chest as his gloved hand firmly gripped her face. The glint of the scalpel reflected from the dim light from the street – once more that wet sound of metal on flesh could be heard, but this time more gentle; less tearing and more care went into the act.

He stood after a moment, looking down at the sapphire beauties he'd cut from her head now resting in his palm. He produced a jar from his long black coat and gently placed the eyes within, then placed the jar back into his coat. A long, firm meow caught his attention as a cat rubbed against his leg then looked up to him with one blue, and one green eye before releasing another long meow at him. He smiled, and knelt down allowing the fluffy grey cat to lick the blood from his gloves.

"You did good, my friend." He said in a low, gruff tone. "Now go and find me another prize – our work has only just begun." The man continued, then stood to walk past the cat back in the direction the woman had originally come from.

He left her there – fourteen stab wounds to the chest, and her eyes surgically removed from her sockets. Stuffed into her mouth was a card – a strange card with equally strange designs on it. All that could be sure is that it was not your normal playing card. The crumpled image on the card could be seen as a bat hanging from a fruit. The card itself seemed hand made – poorly at that, but the meaning was obscure to those that didn't know this card for what it was.

"If you'd have gotten on with the letter when I had delivered it this girl might be alive." Simon spoke, his tone soft, but laced with venom.

"Not true – this girl brings forth new, and fresh evidence. An unfortunate sacrifice, of course, but necessary." Her tone was cold – calculated – as she used to be it seemed.

"So… you did read the letter?" Simon questioned, glaring daggers at her.

"Of course I did." She answered simply, turning her eyes to him then. "Does that upset you even more, Simon?" She asked, smirking as the question left her. "Will it upset her highness?" She asked, daring a soft chuckle.

"You forget your station, woman!" He hissed, and in that moment a hand came to rest on his shoulder – Louis stood behind him now glaring his own daggers into the male before him.

"You forget yours, Simon. You came into my home,

throwing your weight about like it means anything at all to me. It must kill you inside to know that a woman doesn't bend to your will." J'ai stated, standing from her chair and walking across the room. "I had more important things to do – the Shadow is still out there, and that overcasts this simple murder case. It's clear someone just fancies himself an artist like the Dollmaker or even the Ripper. The Prim can handle it I'm sure." She said, moving past him to the door.

"The Shadow has once again hit a wall – you've made no further progress other than the fact that it couldn't have left the city, not yet anyway. Not to mention that the Queen herself made this case – the eyeless women – a priority for you to handle. She is already tired of your refusals, as though you have a say." He dared to turn, shrugging from Louis' grip and facing the back of J'ai's head. "It would be a shame to lock you away from that little girl, she seems oddly fond of you after all." He said, noting how the woman had frozen in her place in that moment.

"How dare you – "

"Fine." J'ai cut Louis off in that moment, turning to face Simon finally. "You can tell your Queen that she has gotten her way." He smirked and started walking past her, but stopped when her arm pressed against the doorway, blocking his way forward. "Know that I will remember this though, how you used a child's love to get your way." She lowered her hand and allowed him to leave.

She slammed the door behind him, and heaved a heavy sigh as she crossed her arms. "Madam?" Louis questioned, stepping forward.

"Call for a carriage, tell Caroline she'll have to pick up Hailey from classes this afternoon." She stated and turned back into the room, heading for her bedroom. "I'll be getting ready to leave, you should as well." She said, closing the door to her room behind her.

The carriage arrived, and as always there was a crowd. People mourned the death, but they also clambered around to see it as though it were entertainment. She remembered how they clambered around for her execution – humans calling humans monsters, it was truly laughable. She pushed past the crowd and stepped into the alley – a cat sat quietly atop a trash can as she and Louis walked by. Her eyes watched the feline as it's multi-coloured hues watched her right back, and both only looked away when they were no longer in direct eye contact.

"It's about time." She looked to the gruff man that spoke, his arms crossed as he glared at J'ai impatiently. "Inspector James." He introduced himself then, holding his hand out to her, but of course she ignored it.

"J'ai." She said simply and turned her attention to the crime scene. "Anything of interest here other than the card?" She asked, crossing her arms.

"Her eyes were missing, just like the other three." He said, looking over the blood on the ground. The muggy weather prevented it from drying in the alley. "Seventeen stab wounds, a little more aggressive than the last." He said, and then shrugged. "That cat over there too, caught it licking the blood from the body and as you can see…" He motioned to the small smudged prints of the cat. "Cared little for preserving the evidence." He added, shaking his head.

"Could have killed the cat." J'ai stated simply.

"That's bad luck, miss." He answered, shaking his head quickly.

"Then deal with tampered evidence and don't complain." She said, turning away from the scene. "I'll head to the Prim. I assume the body and evidence was taken there already?" She asked, and he nodded. "Good. Louis let's go." She motioned for him to follow.

Again the cat stared as she walked by, this time J'ai would stop though. She would approach the cat, and it would look up to her. She would reach out, the cat sniffing her hand then pressing it's head against the back of her palm. An odd cat – most animals avoided her like the plague, perhaps because of some side effect from the incident that led her to immortality. Looking at the cat she could tell it was not starving as well, it was too well groomed to be a stray, and far too clean. A glint flashed from around its neck – hidden within the thick fur of its mane was a collar, with a single name carved into the small metal plate.

Gallowholm

"You should go home." She would say then, giving the cat a quick pat on the head. "This is no place for the likes of you." She would add and step away from the feline.

"Never took you for a cat person." Louis stated as they approached the carriage.

"I'm not. Animals don't usually like me – it was a rare opportunity, and I've not pet an animal since I was little." She admitted as she sat in the carriage. "To the Prim – let's get this investigation over with." She huffed, crossing her arms.

"We will find the Shadow, ma'am." Louis said, causing her to look at him. "I know that's what is on your mind. It can't hide forever." He assured her with a kind smile.

"I hope you're right Louis. You saw what it was capable of at its weakest… imagine what it could do with enough time to acclimate to this world and a new body." She said, turning her eyes out the carriage window. "A true monster, Louis." She would say suddenly. "People called me a monster, but I barely shine a light to those that truly go bump in the night."

Chapter Nineteen

We go through every day walking through life with eyes cast forward. The faces of people we pass blurred to our vision – we've stopped paying attention to those around us, to everything around us. It's rare to find those who see, but when eyes finally do meet it's hard to imagine what is actually seen. Ever since Caroline was a girl she saw things, things kids should never see. Spirits, and things that slither along the alleys, and hide among the muck and trash. She has even seen the doors, but she knows well enough never to go through them because what she sees more than anything else are the colours.

Some are vibrant and warm – these people are the nicest to be around. Their positive energies always infectious in a way that only those like her could appreciate, but there were more people out there with cold, and dry energies – these people drone through life, and always seem to be down about something. She was always able to see people for what they were, and for their intentions. This sight kept her out of trouble all her life as she grew up, that is until she came to work for the Mauvais household, and she met the lady of the house – J'ai.

The woman scared her – this much was true, but she learned over time that despite the shadows that surrounded her, she was an oddly kind person. She took care of the people of her household like family, but Caroline could see she harbored such sadness deep within her. Louis was different – in the beginning he was indifferent it seemed, but he was not like anyone she'd ever met before. He had no color, a true neutral, and it was because of the extra work she had to put in just to understand him they fell in love. Now, happily she was married to her sweet Louis, and together they raised a wonderful little girl; though not of their own, they loved the little one nonetheless.

She walked with the little one now – through her tenth year she was already quite knowledgeable; of course she was still a child, but she was cunning and smart when she was out for something. She saw a lot of J'ai turning out in the child, but luckily she had a sweet warmth about the colours that danced about her – she knew little Hailey would grow up into a strong woman. She worried about Wilhelm though – today Louis had told her the man wished to see his daughter; it almost angered her, but she knew that what he had gone through was likely enough to break any man. She could not fault him fully, but in her heart she knew she wouldn't be willing to return the girl after raising her for so long.

"Mama." She turned her eyes down to the little girl next to her. "Is Mr. Goddard a nice man?" She asked looking up to Caroline then.

She paused for only a brief moment. "Of course he is." She answered truthfully.

"Is it true that he is my real daddy?" She asked continuing to keep eye contact.

"Yes, we've always told you who your parents were, Hailey." She said with a light chuckle at the silly line of questioning.

"Why haven't I lived with him then?" She asked, finally casting her gaze downward.

"Mr. Goddard has… been through a lot. He wasn't able to care for you at the time… so we did." She answered as best she could without revealing too much on the matter.

"Am I going to live with him now?" She asked, her voice was quieter.

Caroline paused, looking down at Hailey before kneeling

next to the child. "Do you want to live with him?" She asked, and the child turned her eyes up to Caroline then.

"… No." She said softly.

Caroline smiled and brushed her bangs gently. "Then you will stay as long as you wish." She assured her, standing and offering the girl her hand. "Come on, we have to get home so that I can start making supper." Her eyes would glance down a nearby alley.

Her eyes would lock with that of a cat – eyes mixed with one green and the other blue as it stared right at her. She saw the darkness emanating from it ,and her heart tightened within her chest as she got the same sinking feeling she had when she had first seen the Shadow. Had the entity taken the cat as it's new form? She gasped a breath and picked little Hailey up as she hurried down the path towards the apartment building. Coming through the door she pressed her back to the door and exhaled with a sort of relief as she held Hailey close to her.

"Caroline?" She opened her eyes to see Wilhelm standing in the middle of the stairs. "Are you alright?" He asked, taking a step forward.

He looked nothing like the well dressed, and clean shaven man she knew in the past. Time was not kind to him, and neither was the drink it seemed as it left him somewhat bloated. She would admit that it was nice to see some color to him now rather than what he had been. That was only second to what was at the forefront of her mind at the moment. Had the Shadow found them? She had to tell Louis and J'ai somehow, but… she had no idea where they were, and she dared not leave Hailey alone for even a moment.

"Everything is fine, Wilhelm." She said slowly, placing Hailey down.

Wilhelm looked at her, and Hailey returned his curious gaze before moving closer to Caroline after a moment. He chuckled and rubbed his stubbed chin, then ran a hand through his hair in an attempt to make himself look less disheveled. She found the attempt adorable in a way, and looked down to the girl before nudging her forward gently. She looked up to the woman then back to the man who slowly descended the steps. She took two tentative steps forward, and shyly looked up to the man in front of her before taking a single step back as he knelt down to her level.

"Hello Hailey." He said, gently extending his hand out to her.

"Hello…" She said softly, quietly taking his hand and giving a small curtsy.

He chuckled. "So well mannered. I'm surprised with you being around J'ai so much." He stated, glancing at Caroline who chuckled softly but quickly cleared her throat to mask it.

"Aunt Mauvais is the one that said I should take the classes." She said, Caroline confirming with a nod of her head.

"I'm truly amazed." She said with a smile. "Hailey… you know who I am right?" He asked, and she glanced back to Caroline then before slowly looking back to the man before her.

"You're my daddy." She answered, and his smile slowly grew.

"Yeah – I know that might seem strange since it has been so long…" He trailed off for a moment. "You can call me

Wilhelm, if you'd prefer." He said, and she nodded her head shyly. "If you would like, and if Caroline wouldn't mind... perhaps we can go to the park one day soon?" He asked, looking to her, then following her gaze back to Caroline who simply looked between the two.

"Well... I have to make supper anyway and..." She sighed and looked to Hailey. "Did you bring any work home with you?" She asked and the girl shook her head. "If you would like, you and Mr. Goddard may go now while I cook." She said, stepping past them. "Be back for supper though, both of you." She said locking her gaze with Wilhelm.

"Of course." He watched her go, then stepped forward slightly. "Thank you Caroline." He said, watching her pause.

"No need to thank me, Wilhelm." She said softly and continued up to her's and Louis' own room.

She closed the door slowly, and waited until she heard the two leave the building before she allowed the tears to fall from her eyes. She was afraid – worried that Hailey would want to go with Wilhelm someday. It was selfish, but she didn't want to give the girl up after so many years of caring for her. She opened her eyes, both cast to the ground as she thought for a moment, but then slowly her head tilted as she noticed the shadow on the floor was not hers. Her eyes lifted, and standing in the room in front of her was a man dressed head to toe in black – a thick brimmed black hat covering his face.

He had no color – like Louis, he was devoid of anything that told her what his true intentions might be. She parted her lips to scream but in that moment he waved his hand, and in that moment her throat felt tight, no sound would escape her. She felt his hand grip around her throat as he forced her to look up at him – he grinned, and pressed the index of his opposite hand to his lips as he slowly shushed her. In an instant he and Caroline would be gone, the apartment empty, the balcony window the only thing open. It was the only way in, and the only way out.

Smokey grey would elegantly land on the balcony edge from above. The grey feline would slowly walk into the room of Caroline, and look around carefully before hopping up on a nearby counter. A lamp burned dimly – the cat moved around it before it's tail knocked the lamp to the carpeted floor below. It sat on the counter's edge and stared at the flame, its green eye becoming slightly brighter as the flame grew larger and spread quickly over the carpet and up the walls in an almost unnatural way. The cat jumped to the floor once more and out the balcony window. It jumped up to the railing and gave one final look into the now blazing apartment before jumping down to the alley below with no worry – then scurried off with a long meow as it faded into the city, and Caroline with them.

Chapter Twenty

History repeats – time cycles on a wheel in constant motion. The smoke from the apartment billowed upward, blankets of black smoke against the grey skies of Victoria. The fire raged for several moments before a neighbor finally contacted the proper authorities. Fire police rushed about trying to stop the flames from spreading, but by the time they got there the neighboring apartments had also caught flame. J'ai and Louis had arrived the moment word had reached them – she burst from the carriage staring up at the building with a worried gaze, Louis rushing forward and calling out to Caroline, but was met with only the image of the apartment roof collapsing inward.

"J'ai!" She turned to see Wilhelm rushing to her side, Hailey in his arms as his eyes also fell upon the fire. "What happened?" He asked, unable to look at her in that moment.

"Caroline!" Louis bellowed, moving to the other man. "Tell me my wife is with you!" He exclaimed, tears pooling in his eyes.

"No, she–" His gaze returned to the apartment building.

"No..." Louis muttered, bringing his hands to his face as he turned back to the building. "No – no – no!" He screamed, falling to his knees, his wailing ringing out over the murmur of the crowd growing around them.

It was a pain she'd never seen in him before – a part of him died that day, but it would turn out to not be the last time he would experience that pain. Once the fire was finally put out, it was time to search for the remains, but in the days that followed no remains would be found. There was only a moment of relief, believing she could be alive, but quickly all of our thoughts turned to one thing – the Shadow. The entity was responsible for the fire at the manor; it had looked into Caroline's eyes, and she looked back – she was a threat. How wrong we were from the very beginning.

We had no clue.

"I have a friend, they live in the country and told me I was more than welcome to join them on the train. Hailey and I would be safe away from the city, and hopefully away from the Shadow." Wilhelm spoke softly, he'd cleaned himself up in the days that followed Caroline's disappearance. Life seemed to have breathed into him again.

"You have my blessing. Take care of her." J'ai would speak, looking to the man with a sad gaze. "I am sorry, Wilhelm, for everything." She said, looking down at the sleeping girl on the tattered chair.

A cheap loft at the edge of the city is all they could get – not that they couldn't afford more, but with the string of bad luck following J'ai around when it came to homes not many others would offer her lodging, child or not. The rain beat against the window in the ceiling. She reached out and brushed her fingers through the girl's hair, a gentle smile pulling at her lips. She would exhale softly and step away from the chair, turning for the door then before she would feel Wilhelm's hand wrapped around her wrist.

"I don't blame you – not for any of it. You did your best, and I know that." He said, his eyes telling her he was being honest.

She placed her hand over his, slowly pushing it away. "Not for your wife… everything else." She would look to him, surprise in his eyes. "Everything." She added, and then turned to the door, stopping for only a moment. "Don't miss a thing, Wilhelm. Not a single moment in the rest of her life, because the time you have together is all either of you have now." She finished and finally left them alone.

She was tired of the weight pushing down on her, like a force she had been dragging with her for longer than she cared to realize. The anger, the guilt, the loneliness. She hated all the pressure put on her for the decisions she made because of her own selfishness – her own unwillingness to just let go. She fought death, and the balance of their world – she suffered for it now, and it took this long for her to see it, accept it, and finally feel it. She had to though, now of all times she had to accept it, and see this through to the end.

"Louis." She stepped outside of the shabby building to find Louis leaned against the carriage. His hope of finding Caroline alive had all but gone as he played with the ring on his finger. "Enough of that, we have to finish this case, and then we can finally focus on the Shadow." She said, placing a hand on his.

His gaze turned to her slowly. "I know…" He said softly, lowering his hand to his side. "I'm afraid…" He said suddenly. "I knew she would die before me, but… I didn't think –"

"Don't think like that – don't think of the worst before you know for sure, Louis. Trust me, we will find her." She interrupted him before he could finish the sentence.

Even she didn't want to think of the possibility of Caroline being dead – it would be the first of their true inner circle. Wilhelm's wife was a crack in the door, but Caroline would be the very key to unlock and show them the other side. The reality of their existence, an eternity of loneliness. How quickly that key turned in the days that followed – J'ai would focus on the killing of the women as the Queen had ordered, and Louis scoured the city for anything he could find relating to the Shadow – any hint, anything at all that was strange or out of place in anyone or anything.

Then it happened.
Another body turned up…

It was strange, like a familiar feeling in the air that just made J'ai hesitate as she stared out the window of the carriage to the covered mound left in the alley. Louis was the first out, he didn't even wait as he walked toward the crime scene. J'ai stepped out slowly, a flash of grey catching the corner of her eye as she saw a familiar feline sitting on a stoop just at the entrance of the alley in front of one of the buildings. They made eye contact for a moment, but only briefly before she heard the sound of Louis crying out from the alley.

She turned to see him pushing the officers aside and dropping next to the body. She moved quicker now, stopping only when she saw Louis lift the lifeless body of Caroline into his arms as he slumped down in the alley – she watched him cradle her. Like the other victims she was stabbed multiple times, and her eyes were removed. Unlike the others though, her card was not shoved into her mouth, at least she was spared that indignity. She picked that card up from the dirty ground – it showed the image of a woman's hat, and a golden cup filled with blue fire, a heart at the center. She felt the tacky, cold of Caroline's blood on the back of the card.

She looked to Louis as he sobbed over the woman he loved – she watched him die all over again in that moment. It would turn out to be a part of him he would never get back, no person could recover from such pain. She didn't realize how much it would hurt him though, as it would turn out Louis wasn't as capable of breaking free from the pain like

Wilhelm. After some convincing she finally got him to release the body to the coroner, and that was the last time she would see him. All she would get from him would be a wild glare, a blaming gaze she never expected to get from him. It hurt more than anything she'd ever felt before.

She watched him climb into the carriage and ride off, leaving her there with Primburogh. For the first time since the accident she truly felt alone – all these people walking around her, speaking to her, and at the center of it all she stood alone. Time moved too quickly, and even then she did the most mortal thing she'd done in many years – decided that Louis needed time alone, and that it was better to leave him to it. Hindsight tells us that certain moments in time could have been avoided if only we'd done things differently, perhaps this was one of those moments. That's the problem with hindsight – we only see these options when it is too late.

Somewhere along his ride he'd made the driver pull over. He walked along the canal, eyes red with tears as he thought back on all the times he'd spent with Caroline. The secret glances that led into a not-so-secret affair, dancing, and luncheons together. Starting a family, getting married… it didn't feel like enough. There wasn't enough time – he didn't get enough time. It wasn't fair. In his anger he tore the ring from his finger – their ring. He reached into his pocket and produced hers – he'd taken it from her corpse as he held her in his arms. All he had of her now was this ring, and the memory of her hollowed eyes looking up to him with blood stained tears.

"Caroline…" He whispered her name as he held the rings close to him. "My Caroline." He had no tears left to shed – his heart hurt too much to force more out.

"Louis." He turned suddenly at the unfamiliar voice, his eyes glancing around before turning back behind him, and meeting the gaze of a young man likely no older than fifteen. "I've been watching you." He added, forcing Louis to stand.

"I am in no mood today – if you want to fight I will happily fight right now." He growled at the boy, assuming him for a mugger in that moment.

"I smell the blood of the woman." The boy stated, and Louis' eyes widened.

"Shadow." He hissed, daring a step forward. "You –"

"No, not I." He stated quickly. "I was not interested in the woman." The Shadow walked forward, stopping when he was standing in front of Louis. "I know who was though." He muttered in a playful, sing-song voice.

"Tell me!" Louis exclaimed, clenching his fists.

"Tsk-tsk – so impatient. I'm not just going to give you what you want. I'm stronger now, I've gotten used to these bodies. It took a long time, but perfection doesn't happen overnight." He said, crossing his arms as he stared at Louis.

"You want something in return don't you?" Louis asked, narrowing his gaze.

"Of course I do." The shadow answered, surprisingly honest about his intentions.

"Speak." Louis ordered, crossing his arms in the same fashion as the entity before him.

"While I have perfected the control of mortal hosts I am not without weakness. If they die I will die, at least if I don't find a new host quickly. I wish to make you an offer, one I believe you will like given your current state." The Shadow moved closer. "Be my partner – I will let you use me, and you will maintain control, but…" He trailed off briefly to keep Louis from speaking quite yet. "Every so often I get to take control – a mutual agreement and now that I've learned how to better assert myself into my vessels it is easier to keep them alive and in control of the body most times." He explained, and then smirked at Louis. "Well?" He questioned.

"Why would I trust you? After what you did, I would be a fool." He stated, getting ready to turn away from him.

"I saw the man that went into your marital room, saw him leave with the girl with special eyes." Louis turned his eyes to the Shadow then. "They hunt me too." He could see the question in Louis' gaze. "Her eyes, Louis. She could see things no other could, even me. Remember how she warned you then?" Louis' eyes widened as he slowly understood. "While you have no reason to trust me, know that when we first met I was nothing more than a child in this world." He chuckled. "Wild and out of control. I am far more tamed now." He stated, then held his hand out to Louis. "Let's work together, and together we will exact revenge on those that mutilated your dear Caroline." Louis stared at the hand extended to him.

"What about the body you're already in? What happens to it?" He asked.

"He will be fine – a little lost, but fine. Now quit stalling." He said, waiting with his hand outstretched.

Louis stared for a long time – he wasn't sure. His heart ached and he did want revenge, and with that thought alone it didn't take much else for him to lock hands with the

Shadow. A toothy grin pulled over the Shadow's expression as that bulge appeared in the entity's throat and worked it's way up. That sickly yellow eye, now tinted with a red outline around the pupil, stared deep into Louis' eyes – reflecting his image. There was no fear in the man as he knew what was about to happen – the only thought he had was of Caroline, and how he made this choice not for himself, but for her.

Revenge.

Chapter Twenty-one

It's a strange feeling, being truly on your own, but she couldn't afford to dwell on that feeling now. Louis vanished after that day – she believed he needed time, and time was all they had now, and so she would give him that. She followed a lead given to her by a fresh-faced officer at Primburogh – he told her about a woman that had cards that looked similar to the ones found on the women, and told her that the old woman often did spiritual readings with them. After all she'd seen she truly wouldn't doubt the possibility of fortune telling having some truth to it. She would give the lead a chance.

The rain pelted against her jacket as she looked up to the shambled building – it had the look of an old storefront, one long since abandoned. Candles flickered in the windows, and the sign on the door was turned to open. She pushed the door open, the bell above the door struck as she stepped inside and shook the chill from the rain from her coat. The silence that fell over her once the bell had died down was odd even to her – the whole store gave off a strange energy, as though nothing here was natural to this world. She walked deeper in and came to the counter to find an old man sitting behind the counter – he stared aimlessly as though he were nothing more than a doll placed here by another.

"I'm looking for an old woman that would know something about cards." She said, the man didn't even look at her. She narrowed her eyes and pulled one of the cards from her pocket and held it in front of the man's face. "Do you know what this is?" She asked, and finally his eyes shifted to focus on the image before him.

"Cups." Was all he said, his voice as dusty as he looked. With a rickety arm he pointed to a door hidden away in the back of the room. "Esmeralda will know." He wheezed out before returning to his catatonic state from before.

She stared at the strange man for a short moment before slowly making her way to the back of the room. As she approached the door a tall man stepped out,placing a hat atop his head as he was stepping through the threshold, and for a moment they stopped and locked eyes with one another. He smiled, and gave her a nod before gripping his bag, and walked past her. She noted the initials on the bag as O.Z., but found it unimportant in that moment. Finally stepping into the dimly lit room she saw an older woman sitting in the center of the floor with a strange board in front of her. This place was strange, the strangest she'd ever seen.

"Sit." She turned her eyes down to the old woman sitting before her.

"I do not have time for-"

"You will sit, or you will leave. The choice is yours, Gravedigger." The old woman interrupted her, J'ai narrowed her eyes.

Silently she would sit, the old woman never once opened her eyes to look at her, but instead continued to sit silently in front of her board. She had no idea that such practices went on in the city, right under the queen's nose no less. How had she not seen places like this before? So many years – even before the incident – she lived in this city, and not once had she seen a place like this. Perhaps it was the same as the doors that the Shadow came through, the same Peter and his son were trapped in. Perhaps only those truly looking, or who stumble upon such places can find even shops like this one.

"Show me." Her eyes were open now, milky grey, and devoid of image as she stared blindly upward with her hand outstretched before her.

"How do you know I have anything to show you?" J'ai asked, genuinely curious now.

"Live as long as I have without worldly sight, you begin to see things in other ways. Often things most don't want to be seen." She answered, wiggling her fingers impatiently in that moment.

She reached into her jacket and produced Caroline's card. She paused for a moment to stare at the wrinkled card that was clearly handmade, the dried patch of red at the bottom left of the card pulled her gaze to it. She brushed her thumb over the spot – a part of Caroline was on this card. She knew she shouldn't, but she wanted to know what Caroline's last moments were like – she hoped they were quick. Given the wounds on her body, she doubted a quick death was the case. With a soft sigh she held the card out to the woman – it barely touched her fingers when she let out a hiss and practically slapped it from J'ai's hand.

"Darkness!" She exclaimed, then spit on the floor to her right. "True dark intent went into that tarot." Esmeralda spoke, finally reaching out and picking the card up once more. "I am sorry for the life you lost – I can feel how important the person tied to this card was to you." J'ai narrowed her gaze as she crossed her arms.

"What is it?" J'ai asked, disregarding what she'd said in that moment.

"Cups." She said, placing the card on the board in front of her, running her fingers over it. "The page of cups. It means he has found what he has been looking for all this time." She said, staring upward as though someone were speaking to her.

"What has he been looking for? Who is he?" She asked, leaning forward now.

"He can't see it on his own, not without his other half. The doors." She whispered the last part. "With her eyes he will open the door, and call back to him the other half he lost in the journey here." Her hands began to shake as she pressed harder onto the card.

"Who? What is his name!?" J'ai exclaimed, tired of the word play.

"Gallowholm!" Esmeralda wailed, jerking her hands violently away from the card on the table, and sliding backwards away from her board. "I can see no more…" She spoke, clutching a hand to her chest.

"Who is Gallowholm, where is he? I need to know." J'ai spoke, a hint of desperation in her voice.

"The girl could not tell me, not in time. There was so much she had to show me, and so little time to do it." She said, sliding her hand across a shelf until she came to a glass of water, then took a long drink from the glass.

"Girl…?" J'ai asked, staring now at the old woman, uncaring of the case at this point.

"She had pretty green eyes – she wept blood." She spoke, her voice hoarse as she took another drink.

"Caroline…" J'ai whispered her name, turning her eyes down to the card. "Did…" She paused for a moment, thinking briefly on how crazy what she was about to ask might sound to anyone beyond this room. "Did she show you anything about where they took her, even a glimpse?" She asked, taking the card from the table and placing it back into her jacket.

"I saw nothing – she showed me only a name, and… a cat."
J'ai's eyes widened as it all hit her at once.

The cat – Gallowholm – the name on the collar that was
around the cat's neck. Perhaps it wasn't the cat's name, but
the name of the owner of that cat. She stood, almost falling
back over from not being used to sitting on the floor. The
old woman heard the fumbling about as J'ai quickly
muttered aloud everything her mind was processing –
though it was choppy, and hard to comprehend for anyone
outside her own mind. She reached out and took J'ai's wrist
into her hand, causing the woman to stop and stare down at
her with a confused gaze.

"I have something for you." Esmeralda would speak softly
as she reached up her sleeve, and produced a card similar
to the one's found on the body. "I sense this card is
meaningful to you." She stated, placing it into J'ai's hand.

"What is it?" She asked, staring at it.

It was better made than the ones Gallowholm had been
leaving at his crimes. A black wolf chasing the moon. The
wolf appeared to fly through the stars, chasing the moon
flying through the sky as easily as a bird, but beneath the
wolf was a white outline, a sort of shadow she supposed.
The card meant nothing to her, she didn't understand their
meanings, and to be perfectly honest she did not enjoy that.
She preferred to have an understanding of everything
around her, but this escaped her completely.

"The moon – it represents intuition, shadow, and reflection."
She paused, looking through J'ai with a blind gaze. "You
spend too much time within yourself, secluded from those
you love. You have resigned yourself to your fate, and so
you care not for the passage of time." She would smile and
put J'ai's hand gently. "Understand the shadows, and

illusions you create about yourself, and your life, but do not dwell in their darkness – lest that darkness become you." She said, then returned to sit in front of her board.

"What does that mean?" J'ai asked, and the woman simply smirked.

"Feel the card." She answered, waving her hand in a motion telling J'ai to leave now. She would do just that, and begin to turn toward the door she'd entered through. "Remember, Gravedigger, spending too much time in the dark often leads one to an irrational place of fear." J'ai looked at the strange woman briefly from over her shoulder before quietly continuing out of the room.

She looked down to the card in her hand – she didn't quite understand what even happened in that shop. It was all so strange, more strange than anything she'd been involved in. She pondered on the nickname the old woman had rudely given her, though she would commend her creativity – not a single other soul living in this city had even called her that, not even in the post. Monster was the extent of their creativity. She chuckled softly and slipped the card into the opposite side of her jacket, but the woman's final words continued to play over and over in her mind.

"Spending too much time in the dark often leads one to an irrational place of fear." She repeated the words aloud, noticing only at the end that the carriage she'd arrived in had gone, and the sun was quickly setting.

"I didn't think you were ever going to come out." She turned to the familiar voice – Louis stood leaning against the wall of the alley next to the shop. "I've finished mourning, it's time to kill this animal." She stared at him – he was strangely calm, and she noticed he was no longer wearing his wedding band.

"Louis?" She questioned, but he simply walked past her.

"Come – I know how to find the one that killed Caroline." He stated, and her brows furrowed in confusion.

"Where have you been – how have you found this information so quickly?" She asked, but her questions went unanswered. "Louis, are you certain you're alright?" She asked, and only then did he stop.

"Yes. I'm better than I've ever been, Madam." He answered, keeping his back to her as they continued to walk further down the sidewalk.

"Where are we going?" She asked, keeping her pace just behind him. Something was very strange about how cold Louis had become in such a short time – like a statue almost.

"You will see, we do not have to go far." He assured her.

They walked for several moments, approaching a row of abandoned buildings. The old housing units were coming apart at the seams, a row of shingles sliding from the roof and crashing loudly against the footpath as they passed by. He guided her inside one of the buildings – the layout was similar to the old apartment with a stairwell right at the entrance, and rooms lining each hall that would then lead to another set of stairs. At the top of the stairs was another hall, doors lining this as well – some broken open and emptied, others locked and untouched for years. They would stop at the end of the hall, greeted by a dead end as the two simply stood there for a long moment.

"Louis what is going on?" She asked, crossing her arms.

"There is a door here." He stated, reaching out and brushing his fingers against the old, dirty wall.

"I just see a wall, Louis. Perhaps we should go to the loft and sleep the night off, go back at it tomorrow." She suggested, but he would glance down to her and shake his head.

"Look." He stated, and ripped the old wall paper away revealing a strangely new door with a golden handle. "Peter's door." Louis stated, pressing his hand to the wood of the door.

"How did you know this was here, Louis?" She asked, her eyes narrowing as she watched him. Something was definitely wrong, she could feel it.

"Doors are everywhere, if you know where to go looking for them." He would smirk and grip the handle of the door then. "Do you want to find this killer?" He asked, J'ai nodded firmly. "Do you trust me?" He asked, turning his eyes down to her in that moment.

"I trust you, Louis." She answered, their gaze locking in that moment as the darkness was broken by a stream of light that came from the door as Louis opened it.

Chapter Twenty-two

It was strange walking through these halls, the very same halls that Peter and his son had wandered, the very halls the Shadow itself had crawled out of. She stared at Louis' back as that thought crossed over her – his peculiar behavior was more than enough, and she knew well that in his grief he would jump on any opportunity for revenge. She knew well before they had entered that abandoned flat that her friend was gone – perhaps not gone, but he'd given up, which to her was far worse.

'Oh Louis, what have you done?' She thought as she simply stared at this vessel in front of her.

She followed this entity into this world, this seemingly endless place, and as they walked she took note of how copy and paste everything was. The carpet, the walls, and the strangely bright light that filled every corner, but despite the light, and all the space it was very claustrophobic. She could see how a place like this could traumatize someone. Her eyes would turn from the walls to the back of Louis, who at the same time turned his gaze away from her, though she had caught him briefly watching her from over his shoulder.

"Where are you taking me?" She asked, her tone distant compared to how she would normally speak to Louis.

"We're getting closer." He answered, but stopped at that moment before turning to face J'ai. "You know, don't you?" He asked, his eyes cold as he looked at her. She didn't answer, she simply kept a distance, and a sharp eye on him. "I see. It's still me, J'ai. The Shadow is somewhere inside – it did not force me though." He said, he hated the look of disgust in her gaze, and knew he should feel ashamed.

"Idiot." She said, her tone short and simple. "I'd have expected it from Wilhelm, but you?" She shook her head. "It will take control of you, it will destroy you." She said, fire in her tone as she fought the desire to slap the Shadow right out of him.

"I know that, and that's why I told the Shadow that the only way I would allow it in my body would be if we shared the control, and it only got to take over if I was in danger." He chuckled then. "I can't die, so danger isn't something I have to worry about." She shook her head at his words.

"You really are stupid!" She hissed, taking a step forward. "I guarantee you it will betray you." She stated, and watched as he shook his head.

"It won't, it wants me to protect it." He said, noting the confusion in J'ai's gaze then. "Gallowholm is searching for it, but has no idea that it already escaped the Veil." He paused, staring to the side for a moment as though he was hearing the voice of another. "I'm sorry, him – the Shadow is male." He stated out of nowhere.

"If Gallowholm is looking for *him* then why take the Shadow right to the man?" She asked, crossing her arms. "On top of that, what does he want with the Shadow?" She branched her questions as they stood in the center of the Shadow's territory.

"Gallowholm wants to be whole again – the Shadow is his missing piece. That is why he wants him back. Why would we march in there the way we plan to? Because I want to kill the man that mutilated Caroline with my bare hands." Louis hissed as he turned and continued walking.

"Does the Shadow know why he is killing these girls?" She asked, there was a pang in her heart before asking her follow-up question. "Why Caroline?" She added.

"Eyes are powerful things – it is true when they say eyes are the windows to the soul, but they are much more than just that. Caroline – especially – had a very unique vision. She could see things others couldn't, she could see the doors to the Veil." He stopped in front of one of the doors. "He needed her eyes so that his human vessel could find the right entrance." He turned his gaze over his shoulder. "The cards were just a fun, leftover side effect of his vessel's nature." He added, pointing to the door in front of them in that moment. "This is the one." He said then.

"How can you be sure?" She asked, crossing her arms. "If Gallowholm can't see the doors without someone else's eyes then how can the Shadow?" She asked.

"As I said, the Shadow is his missing half." He looked to J'ai then. "His stronger half." He added reaching out for the handle and pushing the door open.

The two stepped through the door, and were greeted by a strange sight – long red carpeting that extended the length of a hallway of marbled floors and neatly kept white-wash walls. Portraits lined the hall, and J'ai stared in confusion until she came to one particular photograph, and her eyes widened. In the hanging portrait she saw her mother and father – she was eight at the time, and stood beside her mother who held her infant brother in her arms. She hadn't seen this portrait in years – she had forgotten what her family had looked like then.

"What is this place?" She asked, and Louis turned to look at her.

"This is the hall of dead memories." He answered, and she looked back at him then. "That portrait is here because that

199

part of you died. A memory you lost, and like all dead things, ended up here. Even the things we view as minuscule – like a portrait or a memory – die and find themselves collected here in the Veil." He continued forward, and J'ai slowly followed.

"What is the Veil? Is it heaven or hell?" She asked, this place becoming more interesting to her than the task at hand.

"Both." He answered as they walked through the new set of halls. "The true first concept of the afterlife came from some poor fool in the Eastern part of the world, the name of the city escapes me. He was pulled into the Veil much like Peter and his son, but he was lucky enough to witness the wonders and horrors from a safe distance and he interpreted it as a place where the good go to be reborn and the evil go to be eternally tormented." He shook his head. "The Veil doesn't care about good or evil, that is a human ideal. How does one even begin to really define good, or evil?" He chuckled. "The Veil simply just exists. Exists, and feeds, and thrives. It is both a plane of existence, and a living thing." He said as they continued through the halls.

"Seems complicated." J'ai stated as she looked at the other portraits lined the halls – memories from other places, of other people. "It seems it has no concept of time either." She said to herself.

"The Veil is everywhere all at once. It exists in all timelines of every reality." She arched her brow then.

"So in theory we could walk through a door and end up in a whole other world? In another time period all-together?" He looked back at her then.

"Anywhere, in any time." He nodded, and J'ai made an

impressed expression.

"It's so complex… a world of it's own that exists simply to exist. It's not exactly an afterlife – it's a pathway." She said, and Louis nodded.

"Yes. You just have to know how to navigate through it." He then pointed to another door – this one was different from the others they'd seen. It was old, and cracked. "However even this place has it's dangers, and it's own way of warning wanderers away from them."

J'ai nodded slowly. "Note to self: avoid old looking doors." She turned and smirked to Louis then, who returned the expression with a light smirk.

He turned toward an adjacent hall – a hall J'ai hadn't even seen. "This way, we're getting closer." Louis stated and the two continued.

"We can stop for now."

J'ai looked at the man sitting at the table across from her. He had turned the cassette off, and began to rummage around in his bag. She sat at the small wooden table with a cigarette dangling between her fingers as she watched him with silent annoyance. She wore a white button down, the sleeves rolled to her elbows, and black dress pants and shoes, her left leg crossed over her right. She rolled her eyes and took a long drag from her smoke as she turned her eyes to look out the window, looking out over the city that was still ever growing.

"I told you that you would run out of tape before the end." She said, taking another drag from the cigarette.

"You did. Honestly, I'm amazed myself." The man across from her chuckled. "Your adventures are some wonderful ones. Dark and macabre as they are, they are real and true, and not to mention the knowledge of the Veil you have. Astounding." He said, his tone was one of astonishment and wonder – not the one of horror she expected.

"You are a strange man, Mr. Ollivanders." She said, watching him rummage through his case looking for more tape.

"Please, Ozwald. My father was Mr. Ollivanders. A-ha!" He exclaimed, producing another cassette tape. "I knew I had a back-up." She watched him replace the tape, and once again hit the play button. He locked his fingers together, and looked to her with a natural smile that painted his face. "Now, how about we skip ahead a little – to where you and Louis have left the Veil and confronted Gallowholm." He said, and J'ai leaned forward to press the cigarette out in the tray in front of her.

"When we finally left the Veil… we ended up in some shack in the countryside. Old and falling apart – the windows were boarded up and the place reeked of death." Her eyes stared forward, staring at the table as though she were right back there at that point in time. "That damn cat was there, sitting on the table. Staring at us as we walked into the room through a door that originally led to a storage closet I assume. It was like the cat knew, or was expecting us." She sighed and pulled another cigarette from a pack in her pants pocket – she lit it, and inhaled slowly. "Not even I was ready for what was going to happen that night in that countryside shack." She exhaled the smoke slowly as she finished her sentence.

Chapter Twenty-three

It was an interesting turn of events – J'ai had not been ready to walk through a whole new world, but she hadn't been ready for a lot of things. A lot of life, and her perspective on it had changed ever since the accident – she never expected this much change though. The world was not as she believed it to be, it was not as anyone believed it to be. It had become abundantly clear that there were people that knew, and kept it a secret from those beneath them. Back then though she would have never believed Louis would have given his body up to a being like the Shadow, yet here they were. The unbelievable became real, yet in reality she should have already seen all of this, but she remained oblivious to it by choice – thinking her and Louis' circumstance was purely coincidental.

How foolish she was.

They stepped into a dark room – from what she could see it was an old house. The walls were moldy, and the floorboards seemed to have been weathered from rain dripping through the roof. She peered from one of the boarded windows, and was able to see that they were somewhere in the countryside – where exactly she couldn't tell. Louis continued moving through the house, J'ai followed as she took in the new environment they were in. The possibilities, scientifically, that could be accomplished with the Veil were endless – travel would become so simple, but the dangers of pulling something through with you… those dangers were far too great in comparison to the benefits.

From beneath the table a streak of grey, followed by a loud hiss caused the two to freeze as they heard the sound of the cat running up the stairs. They looked to one another, and nodded. Both silently agreed at that moment that they would see this through to the end. J'ai produced a knife from beneath her jacket, and readied herself for some kind of confrontation. Louis was ready in his own way, physically able to hold his own against something like the Shadow – surely he could hold his own against this Gallowholm. They moved up the stairs and down the hallway, checking rooms as they progressed through the upper level of the house, the floor whining beneath their footsteps.

"Gallowholm!" Louis cried out bounding down the hall, his fist clenched and ready. "Face me you cowardly bastard!" He bellowed, kicking one of the doors in.

The cat scurried from the room with a violent hiss as it's claws fought to find traction on the floor. As Louis kicked doors in, and loudly called out for their prey, J'ai turned her eyes on the cat running through the house to find a place to hide. She tilted her head, following the cat into a room down an opposite hall. She pushed the door open slowly, the darkness in the room cracking away more and more as the door floated open further. From the shadows a streak of silver flashed, then a pressure hit her shoulder. She looked down to see the hilt of a small knife protruding from her arm. Her eyes snapped back in time to see another one coming for her – she moved to the side and watched it hit the wall next to her.

"Louis!" She called out as a tall man dressed head to toe in black burst from the room, grabbing her by the lapel of her jacket. "You must be Gallowholm." She spoke in a low tone, reaching up suddenly and managing to pull the knife from her shoulder, and quickly stabbing him in the leg.

The man bellowed out, and quickly gripped J'ai by the face, lifting her from the ground. He used his free hand to remove the blade from his leg, and quickly stabbed J'ai in the neck, dropping her the moment the blade pierced her flesh. The man turned, his single emerald-green eyes glinted as he stared right at Louis. It was as quick as a flick from the man's wrist, and a blade was flying right at Louis – he moved quickly. He was much faster now with the Shadow a part of him, had he known maybe he would have taken this offer sooner. It took more than several moments for J'ai's wound to close, and for her to wake up again. She sat up, slightly dazed before she looked forward. She saw Louis lunge at the man, and immediately be grabbed and tossed through a door to the left.

She stood slowly as Gallowholm wrapped his hand around Louis' throat, but Louis was a lover of knives as well. A blade slipped out from his jacket sleeve, and he smirked as he shoved the knife into the man's gut. He grunted, and swiftly punched Louis in the face before stumbling back and slowly pulling the blade from his stomach. Louis jumped up and grabbed the man's hand, stopping him from pulling it out, and the two struggled. His blood hand raising and managing to shove a finger in Louis' eye, and causing him to cry out. He removed the blade from his gut and reared back, getting ready to stab Louis in the back when he felt something sharp plunge into his lower back.

"For Caroline." J'ai said coldly.

She pulled the knife from his back and stabbed the man several more times before he made a move to hit her, stumbling as he made the attempt. He'd lost a lot of blood, and like the Shadow it seemed it didn't have the awareness to understand it couldn't survive in a normal human body. Louis kicked his feet out from under him, grabbing the knife he was about to stab him in the back with and began to stab Gallowholm over and over again in the chest. Panting he sat on the other man's chest, blood dripping down his cheek as he turned to look to J'ai.

It was over.

"Was it really over?" Ozwald asked, keeping his eyes locked with J'ai as she took a long drag from her cigarette.

She stared silently out the window, her eyes were distant as she looked out over the city. Time moves forward, but as it seems not much changes when it comes to people. As predictable as ever. "Why do you want to know about any of this? You obviously know how it really ended." She said, not bothering to look at him as she spoke.

"I know the version that was officially told. The version edited by the Empire, the unedited record was sealed a long time ago. You would know, you tried to get them." He said, and pressed play on the recorder again. "Are you ready to keep going?" He asked, and J'ai sighed heavily.

"It happened too fast for either of us to realize what was even going on. Louis, soaked in bloody revenge, looked to me as though to ask if that was really it. Like he expected it to be harder." She swallowed back the pain that began to rise up in her.

Louis stood and moved towards J'ai then, the Shadow would be a part of him forever now, but maybe that wasn't a bad thing. He was still Louis after all, and she could see it in his eyes – Caroline was gone, but vengeance was sweet for him. There was a wet sound, and a pressure in J'ai's chest – she watched as Louis' eyes grew shocked, and slowly he looked down. She followed his gaze in that moment, and saw a long, sharp, and fleshy object protruding from her chest, and stabbing into Louis. Her eyes looked up to him again, and his hand reached up to grip the tendril but it reacted quickly, spreading and wrapping around his entire body to keep him in place, and the same happened with J'ai as the two were suspended into the air in their strange fleshy cocoons.

J'ai struggled, and Louis did the same, but it was clear that neither had the strength to break their bonds. "J'ai, it's Gallowholm!"

In her struggle she looked to see the body of the man. "He's dead, how is he doing this?" She asked, and a light chuckling filled the room.

"Now now, you think that fool had all my power?" She looked around the room, but saw no one else.
No one but the cat. "You." She hissed, and the laugh echoed from the cat's maw as it approached the body of it's puppet on the floor. "You're Gallowholm!" She exclaimed, struggling harder only to have her prison tighten around her body.

"Stop wriggling, you're only making things worse for yourself." The cat spoke as it moved to tear the eye from it's human, swallowing it and causing the blue eye of its own to turn green once again. "It's good to be whole again." He said, and then turned his eyes up to Louis. "Almost whole." He added, jumping up to a bookshelf so that he was eye level with Louis then. "What a strange body for you to choose as your host." He said, sitting in front of him. "Odd for you to allow him to keep his mind as well – you're usually the more violent one." He said, and watched as Louis' left eye slowly rolled to the back of his head.

It rolled back all the way, and when it turned fully in his skull it came back up a sickly yellow shade. "At least... I was able to find a productive.... host." The Shadow spoke through Louis – it was the truth when Louis said they would share the body.

Gallowholm hissed, flicking his tail in annoyance. "This body serves me just as well as yours does you." He said, the Shadow laughed.

"You're a cat, you've got no thumbs and no rights within society. At least with my body I'm not limited to things I can do." Gallowholm narrowed his eyes as the Shadow spoke. "I noticed that you can only focus full power on one thing, two of these prisons is too much for that small body to handle, and dividing yourself like this weakens you." He stated and quickly snapped himself free of his prison. His arm shifted and stretched, turning into another mouth, open and ready to devour the cat. "You will be the one eaten this time!" The Shadow hissed.

It happened too fast for anyone to realize what even transpired, the fur on the cat's body stood straight and became sharp as blades. The cat's body shot forward, impaling Louis' body, and specifically through his left eye – the Shadow's eye. The cat's head stretched out, mouth growing open with razor-blade teeth piercing into Louis' abdomen and tearing him open. It bit him several times, tearing his insides out as though it were a person digging through luggage. Finally it began to pull at something black, tearing it violently from Louis' body and swallowing it whole. Louis was dropped, his form bouncing against the floor.

"Finally, I am whole again." He watched J'ai run towards Louis, and lift him into her arms slightly.

His body began to shift into a mass of black until finally it took the shape of the dead man in the room behind them. Dressed head to toe in black he stared down at Louis and J'ai, lifting his hands to look down at them. There was something new mixed into his body with him, something other than the Shadow. Yellow-green eyes turned to Louis and J'ai – she tried desperately to get him to stand, to heal but his body was not acting as it normally would. He wasn't healing, he would not live. He understood now – the part of him others called the Shadow had memories of these two.

Immortals. Dangerous. He moved forward, his arm turning into a blade as he approached them, but then the door to the closet behind them burst open, two arms reached out grabbing J'ai – she gripped onto Louis and the two disappeared inside the door.

J'ai landed in the Veil, Louis in her lap, and she turned her eyes up to see the strange man from the gypsy shop. "That was a close one." He said, his tone oddly calm as he snapped his finger and the door he'd pulled them through disappeared.

"Who –"

"No time, your friend is dying." He interrupted her, pointing to Louis then.

Her eyes shifted back to the man in her arms, he brought his hand up and gripped her forearm, looking up to her with his one remaining eye. "I can't, breathe…" He gasped out in a whisper. "J'ai…" Tears streamed from his eye as he looked up to her. "It hurts." He whispered, and she gently wrapped her arms around him.

"Louis – you're going to be fine. You'll slip away, and just come back like before." She said, staring at him with worry.

He shook his head. "I felt it… go." He said, finding it hard to speak. "Tore it… from me." He brought his

"Tore it from you?" She questioned, and he began to cough, and shake violently.

"His immortality." The other man spoke, and J'ai looked up to him. "Oh, I'm Ozwald. Sorry." He said, taking a step back. "I forget death is a sensitive thing sometimes." He added before turning away from them.

"J'ai—" She looked down to him, taking his hand in hers. "Will she be... here?" He asked, his eyes looking somewhere in the distance. "Caroline?" He added, his grip was loosening.

"I... "

She reached across the table and turned the recorder off. "Hey!" Ozwald exclaimed, picking the little machine up from the table protectively.

"You know the rest of what happens. I'm done telling the story." J'ai stated, standing suddenly, and grabbing her jacket from the chair.

"Gallowholm is still out there." Ozwald stated, watching her throw her jacket on and head for the door.

"That isn't my problem." She stated.

"You're still bound to this country, whether or not Her Majesty is alive." He added, and this time she turned to him.

"Then send your armies after me – hunt me down, lock me away and never let me see the light of day again! I do not care!" She hissed, storming back towards him. "There is nothing this country can do to me, nothing it can take from me that has not already been done to me. I've lost everything, everyone I've ever loved or cared about if gone." She sighed softly, staring down at him. "I do not fear this country or it's Queen, Mr. Oleander." She stated, and then arched her brow when he began to chuckle.

"That is what I like to hear." He stood then, and put the recorder in his bag. "I believe you misunderstand me – I do not work for this country, nor do I serve it's queen." He said with a chuckle.

"Who are you then? What do you want from me – why do you want to hear my story?" She asked, throwing her hands up. "Why after all these years seek me out and make me relive all of this?!" She questioned, gripping the edge of the table as she looked at him.

"I wanted you to remember the feeling of being alive. You've been wandering through life like the walking dead. Like Wilhelm." He looked down with a soft sigh, then quickly back up. "What did happen to that little girl?" He asked, tilting his head curiously.

"Left the country, went to some school overseas. She is either very old or very dead by now." She said with a soft sigh of her own. "You didn't really answer my question – not fully that is." She said, crossing her arms over her chest.

"You're a strong woman, you've been on the other side as I have. I think you would be perfect to travel with me for a while." He said, standing in front of her then. "I do work similar to what you did, though I don't work with any degree of law." He would smile then, and extend his hand out to her. "If you have the time we can talk about this arrangement fully over some dinner." He said, waiting for her to make her move.

She smirked, and slowly took his hand in hers. "I have all the time in the world, Mr. Oleander."

                              The End.